JOE GENTILE - EDITOR-IN-CHIEF

DAVE ULANSKI - ART DIRECTOR

GARRETT ANDERSON & LORI G - EDITORIAL

GREG GASS & MIKE REYNOLDS - GROUND CONTROL

KATHLEEN O'BRIEN - WEB MASTER

JOE GENTILE & DAVE ULANSKI - PUBLISHERS

moonstonebooks.com

FORWARD

The cut of Wyatt Earp's life across the American history is as indelible as the swath of the Colorado River through the Arizona landscape. With every passing year, the Grand Canyon burrows a little deeper and reveals a fraction more of the tertiary truth that lies beneath the surface. Similarly, as time goes, the fundamental truths about the life and times of Wyatt Earp see daylight for the first time and are, to those who appreciate them, as spectacular and mesmerizing as the walls of the canyon at sunset.

It's sticky business to dive into the historical world of "Earpiana" though. Depending on your perspective, Wyatt Earp was either profane or profound. For the legend of Wyatt Earp, lawman, will forever inspire the bold and capture the imagination of the willing. The mythical visage of Wyatt Earp, hero, will forever confound the curious and infuriate the un-believer. The essential character of Wyatt Earp, the man, presents another proposition altogether. As it was in his heyday, you either like Wyatt Earp or you don't. Interestingly even today, nearly 80 years since his death, Wyatt Earp is a man to be reckoned with. He will remain so.

It is Wyatt Earp's character attributes, wanderlust and fearless nature that spur the debate, create controversy and pit brother against brother in arguments that no one will ever definitively win. Yet, the debate rages on in historical circles. Those who attempt to write about Wyatt Earp on a historically accurate platform often become embroiled in bitter finger pointing and accusations from other writers who would like to lay claim to certain facts as their own. The truth is, there are only so many archival pieces of paper to go around, and sooner or later someone is going to play in someone else's sandbox.

Wyatt Earp's actions have been vivisected in works ostensibly meant to debunk lore, ad-nauseam. To a word, they all lambast Hollywood for its perversion of history in the name of entertainment. Some digress from their historical perspective into pure character assassination vis-a-vis moral judgments and Victorian ideals. They apply modern values to a time when upholding the law among ruthless characters was not the science it is today. The fact that Wyatt gambled, married a whore or two, made deals with scurrilous characters and was out to make money is un-arguable. The fact that he took the law into his own hands with reckless abandon at points in his life is also without question, and generally without contempt. The fact is, Wyatt stood on feet of clay, but he stood tall.

There is a likeness in the young Wyatt Earp, and a great many of our western heroes, to the celebrities of today. They were boys coming to manhood in a hurry. Their lives were replete with money, politics, spin-doctoring and jockeying for position. They were the rock stars of their day and lived as such. Yet the detractors are indignant in their bent to "prove" something regarding Wyatt Earp's humanity. Interestingly, Wyatt never set out to be the extraordinary figure he has become. Had Urilla Sutherland lived, I doubt Wyatt Earp's name would have ever been the subject of writings and films, scholarly and otherwise, that detail, albeit with great poetic license, his doings on one side of the law or the other. Nevertheless, he became a man among men in history, and we are better for it.

Yet there is always this controversy about whether he was a good guy or a bad guy. There is a great dichotomy between historical accuracy and exciting, Buntline Special-wielding heroics we've all come to know and love from the screen. Further, there is controversy about who got it right. Like the man himself, we all come to our own conclusions about who has captured the man best in their works of film or literature.

A prime example of this paradigm of truth is most evident in the saga of two recent films, *Wyatt Earp* and *Tombstone*. The story of how these two films got on the big screen is epic itself and would fill at least as many pages as Justice Riders endwells. These films underscore the dichotomy of truth versus fiction when it comes to Wyatt Earp, or history itself, for that matter. Hollywood has a long history and reputation for poetic license and expansion of facts to serve its own purpose. At every turn, when it comes to the subject of Wyatt Earp, it feels compelled to aggrandize heroics and sublimate humanity, even if his humanity and the drama therein might be a better story.

Summarily, Kevin Jarre, who is in my estimation one of the most brilliant writers around, had penned a masterpiece of a script. It was fascinating, captured the language of the time, and blended accuracy and myth as definitively as could be attempted in the space of a two-hour film. It summed up the events leading up to -- and following -- the gunfight in the vacant lot behind the OK Corral with heroism and reality. It was not only the best script involving Wyatt Earp I had ever read, it was the best modern day script about anything I had ever read. Most every actor in Hollywood agreed. The script would attract A-List talent for only small fractions of their normal fee. Of the 30-some-odd meaty roles in the film, many were played by people who were accustomed to starring roles. In *Tombstone* they might have been lucky to have 5 lines. I felt fortunate to have been cast at all, and relished every second of my four months on the set playing a cowboy who was famous for running out on the gunfight at OK Corral.

Tombstone, like its namesake, became the most perilous film set of 1993. Kevin Jarre was relieved of his directorial debut a month into shooting, and producers scrambled for money to finish the film. The script was brutally edited by several hired gun writers who "punched it up" for action and the love story between Wyatt and Josephine. Eventually the money was found and the production rolled on through the heat of the southern Arizona summer under the direction of George Cosmatos. The budget eventually was finalized at $25 million. The film grossed $56.5 million domestically and has become a huge favorite of a vast audience worldwide. Had the original script survived, I suggest it may have been an Oscar caliber film.

Meanwhile Lawrence Kasdan and Kevin Costner, Oscar caliber filmmakers and heroes of mine, were enjoying a budget of $63 million and the company of buffalo on the landscapes of New Mexico, Montana, etc. while shooting their Wyatt Earp film. The word on the street was that this film would be the definitive Wyatt Earp story. Knowing what Costner had done with *Dances with Wolves*, I sometimes wondered if the decision to cast my "big break" lot with *Tombstone* had been noble but un-wise. Eventually, Kasdan, et al. would bring to the screen a comprehensive story with a huge cast.

Wyatt Earp, the film, encapsulated the life of Wyatt Earp, the man, like no other film ever had, with a fairly poignant degree of accuracy. Costner's performance, in my estimation, probably best captured the essence of the true laconic nature of Wyatt Earp. Nevertheless, the public found the film "boring" and the film grossed $25.0 million.

Heroics and action had again won over accuracy in the battle of these two films. The irony lies in the fact that for the second time in the 20th century, the life story of Wyatt Earp was a flop.

The first time it bombed was in the 1920's when it was told by the man himself to "Hollywood." Wyatt sat with studio heads in the 1920's and was informed that he needed to "punch it up" a little because audiences weren't interested in anything that wasn't heroic. I can imagine Wyatt sitting there in front of a suit, Tom Mix at his side, hearing that his life story wasn't interesting or heroic, and how the aging pugilist might have felt the need to draw blood once again. Had Wyatt been a little less serious and more given to fame-seeking, he might well have seen his life played out on screen before his death. That was not Wyatt's nature, though, and he was relegated to telling his story to his nurse, John Flood, who was at his side as he succumbed, over time, to prostate cancer. Wyatt died an un-heroic death, nearly destitute, two weeks short of his 81st birthday.

So, how do we resolve the conflict of truth versus fiction while maintaining reverence for this great American life? We continue to ask questions.

In all these examinations, films and writings about Wyatt, the bullet holes always wind up in the front of his enemies. The fact that Wyatt was an honorable fighter is for the most part, a given. Yet we are left with questions about the real history, questions about the timeline, questions about Wyatt's motivations and thinking. It is asking these kinds of questions that spurs those courageous enough to tackle the subject of Wyatt Earp to sit in front of a keyboard and to try once again to provide a story that makes sense, or at least a story that is interesting. Too often, the Character of Wyatt Earp has been supplanted to the need of Hollywood to create a more compelling story, when the story of how it really was, the story of how he felt and the story of a man carving out a life, would be grist for everyone's soul.

Like all those men in history of whom we catch glimpses in furtively dashed records of noteworthy episodes, we wish for more. More of the real man, more of the normal moments that compose the vast majority of an authentic life. We wish for the rudiment and essence of character. This longing perhaps points to the need to understand how one's own life squares to the life of other ordinary men in an extraordinary time or in difficult circumstances. I suggest that our own moments of greatness are impacted and influenced by the examples set for us in what we can glean from an incomplete record of who those men really were.

To Richard Dean Starr's credit, he has escaped the morass of historical writing. He has embraced fiction, asked "what if", landed on a compelling amalgam of adventure, possibility and character development, and has melded it all into an unexpected and swift western tale. Like all works that endeavor to capture the essence of character, he has found both profound and profane pieces of Wyatt Earp, the man, and has set them squarely on the canyon wall for all to examine and hopefully, to enjoy.

—— *Wyatt Earp*

Wyatt Earp is the talented actor who portrayed Billy Claibourne in the classic film Tombstone, *and a direct relative of the legendary lawman. A full biography appears at the end of this book.*

WYATT ★ EARP
★ THE JUSTICE RIDERS ★

WRITTEN BY
RICHARD DEAN STARR

ILLUSTRATED BY
DAN DOUGHERTY

EDITED BY
JOE GENTILE

COVER ILLUSTRATION BY
DAVID PALUMBO

COVER & BOOK DESIGN/PREPRESS BY
ERIK ENERVOLD
SIMIAN BROTHERS CREATIVE

August, 1879

It was just after noon on a sweltering Kansas day when Wyatt Earp made his way across Dodge City's dusty Front Street, the letter he had received just an hour before clenched in his right fist.

As he entered the barbershop two doors down from the Long Branch Saloon, the proprietor, Big Tom Walker, took one look at his face and nodded a perfunctory greeting. "Afternoon, Wyatt," he said carefully. "In for a shave?"

Wyatt inclined his head in return but didn't speak. Slipping into the one open chair, he stared down at

the partly crumpled envelope. The contents of the letter inside were weighing heavily on his mind, and the truth be told, the damned thing felt like it weighed a thousand pounds.

"Be right with you then," Walker said, turning back to his current customer.

The man occupying the only other chair in the shop bent his head enough so that he could see around Walker's substantial rear end. "Hello, Wyatt," he said cheerfully. "You look a bit distracted, if I do say so myself."

"Sheriff, I need you to hold still so's I don't cut your throat," Walker said irritably, "if you don't mind." "I'll try to oblige you, Tom," the man said with a slight grin, "considering I'll have need of my throat for a few years yet."

"Can't imagine what for," Wyatt said grumly. "All you Masterson's do is talk and talk. Maybe if Tom slit your throat you'd shut the hell up for a bit."

"Oh, I doubt that would stop me for long," Bat Masterson said. "As you say, I do love to talk. Speaking of which, looks to me like you got some bad news, Wyatt. Anything I should know about?"

Wyatt considered the question. At the present time he and Bat were splitting the duties of Sheriff for Ford County. While the two men were close, Wyatt wasn't sure this was the kind of thing he wanted to share

with anyone, except maybe his brothers -- and at the moment they were too far away to be of any help.

"Nothing that concerns the county," Wyatt said shortly. "It's personal." He took a deep breath. "Although it does look like I might be heading out for a spell, Bat."

Masterson turned his head so fast that Walker had to lift the razor blade up suddenly to keep from slicing the side of his face.

"Heading out? Where to?"

"Like I said," Wyatt replied. "It's personal."

And it was. He stared down at the return address, which was printed in the strong, even hand of the priest named Father Pedro. It had been a long time since he had heard from the old man, and frankly, he'd never expected to again.

He sighed. It wouldn't be right to just ride out of town without giving Masterson some kind of explanation.

Wyatt glanced over at Walker. "Hey, Tom," he said, you mind stepping out for a minute?"

Walker paused for a moment and then nodded. "Sure thing, Wyatt. Been wanting to get out and roll me a smoke anyhow."

After the portly barber was gone, Bat sat up in the chair and swung his feet to the floor. "Okay, Wyatt,"

he said, "You've got my attention. Why the sudden need to leave town?"

"Someone I used to know," Wyatt said, "and a debt I thought was paid." He held up the letter. "Seems it's not."

Masterson studied his friend carefully. "It must be one hell of debt to put you on the trail like this with no warning. Anything I can do to help?"

Wyatt thought about that for a moment. Considering their history together, Masterson being there was the next best thing to his brothers. Or Doc Holliday; but Doc was gone, too, and God only knew where, probably dealing Faro somewhere. He'd turn up sooner or later, but not soon enough to help him fix this mess.

Not that it mattered, really. Wyatt suddenly realized he had no business asking any of them to help settle a debt which was his alone to pay. Like it or not, this was something he was going to have to handle himself.

"You're needed here, Bat," Wyatt said finally. "This is my fight. But there is something you might be able to help me with."

"You know I'll do what I can, Wyatt. Just give me the word."

"That's why I asked Tom to step out," Wyatt admitted, "because what I'm asking you to do could draw some unwanted attention. There's a particular Apache I'm going to need on this ride, Bat, but I need to keep

his involvement quiet."

Masterson looked puzzled. "What's so special about one Apache? You could just ride up to half the tribes out here and talk with whoever you wanted. Hell, you've done it a hundred times before."

"That won't work," Wyatt said, "for a couple of reasons. First off, like I said, I need to keep this quiet. Not all the tribes are at each other's throats these days, you know that. In fact, some of 'em talk *too* damned much. But that's not the real problem. In order to get to this specific Apache, you'll have to call in some markers from your Army contacts."

Bat chewed on his lower lip for a moment. "Just *which* Apache are we talking about here?"

"Geronimo," Wyatt said. "I need to meet with him, Bat, and soon."

There was a moment of shocked silence. Then Masterson said, "What in the hell do you want with him? Last I heard, he surrendered and was living on the San Carlos reservation outside Fort Apache."

"You and me both know life on a government reservation will never suit that old man," Wyatt said. "Besides, those Army markers you're owed could actually get him off San Carlos. This concerns him, Bat, and I need his help."

Masterson considered Wyatt's request. Finally he shook his head and grinned. "Wyatt Earp and Geronimo -- that'd be quite a sight. Too bad I won't be there to see it. I owe you one, Wyatt. Hell, more than one.

I'll send word to a Colonel I know at Fort Apache. He's got the authority to take Geronimo off San Carlos. But I'm warning you, I can't guarantee that son-of-a-bitch will want any part of this -- and I'm not talking about the Colonel."

"I'm obliged to you, Bat," Wyatt said.

Both men stood up. For a moment there was an awkward, yet strangely comfortable pause, the kind which often occurs when two male friends are preparing to part ways.

Then Masterson cleared his throat and said, "Dodge City's going to be a lot slower without you."

" Don't you worry about that," Wyatt said. "It may not be long before we see each other again. Last week I got word from Virgil that things down Arizona way are picking up. He's found himself a town he says is mostly peaceable but growing fast. I'm heading that way after I swing back here to pick up Mattie. Maybe you could come along."

Masterson considered the idea for a moment. Then he said, "I have to admit, things have gotten a bit predictable around these parts. What's this little paradise called?"

"Tombstone," Wyatt said, "if you can believe it."

"Well, you're right about one thing," Masterson said. "It does sound peaceable. Maybe a little *too* much."

Night had long ago fallen on the desert by the time Wyatt finally staked out his horse and set up camp on a lonely hilltop less than two days ride out of Santa Fe, New Mexico.

The air was thinner and quite a bit colder than he remembered from his last visit, so he worked harder and faster than usual to get a good fire going. Once the flames were hot enough, he started some coffee and settled down on his blanket.

It had been three days since he had left Dodge City with little or no explanation to the rest of the townsfolk. At his request, Bat Masterson was watching out for Mattie, but that had not kept his wife from shrieking as if he were heading off to the gallows when she heard that he was leaving.

He had tried to explain that he would be back in a few weeks, maybe less, but still she screamed, carrying on like a sick cat while he loaded up his gear. It took three women and more laudanum than he cared to think about to put her down for the night.

At dawn, Wyatt had ridden out of Dodge City without bothering to say goodbye to her. Mattie hadn't been right in the head for a long time and he knew that waking her wouldn't have done anyone any good.

He shook his head at the memory and stared out past the fire into the night. From his high vantage point the desert was draped in obsidian darkness. Even the stars, which glistened like the facets of an amethyst geode, did not provide enough light to see more than half a dozen yards.

Ordinarily, he would not have camped in such a high spot or allowed his fire to be seen for miles, nor would he have burned it so bright or for so long. But this particular flame, much like the place that he had chosen to camp, was designed to *ensure* he was seen. Without the fire on the hilltop, it was entirely possible that the men he was there to meet might miss him completely. It was, after all, a mighty big desert -- especially after the sun went down.

Taking another sip of strong black coffee, he pulled his pocket watch out of his vest and popped open the lid. Tipping it toward the firelight, he could just make out the fine hands and thin Arabic numerals on the face.

Wyatt had no doubts about the lateness of the hour. Many pocket watches kept poor time, but not this one. It was a Hampden model, the preferred timepiece of professional railroad men. It had been given to him by a grateful conductor whom he had extricated from a bad mess the year before. When wound properly it kept time accurately down to the minute, which meant that Geronimo and his escort were running mighty late.

If they didn't show up soon, it would be time for concern. Having the Apache with him on this ride was a crucial part of the plan he had been formulating since leaving Dodge City.

In the fire, a pitch knot exploded with a dull pop. A brief shower of sparks danced on the tips of the flames before dying away. Wyatt closed the watch and slid it back into his pocket.

The sooner his guests showed up the quicker he could kill the fire. From long experience, Wyatt knew that at night, men were the high desert's most dangerous creatures. Any one of them might see his fire and take an unhealthy interest in his affairs.

He brushed his fingers absently over the Colt New Army double action revolver strapped in a holster to his right leg.

It wasn't a particularly conscious act. Checking for the gun's presence had, over the years, become habit and a life-saving one at that. If anyone came upon him that night with larceny in their heart, he knew he would plug them with the same decisiveness as he would a rabid dog.

Somewhere off to his right he heard a familiar sound in the brush. Setting his coffee cup down carefully beside the fire, he put his hand alongside the Colt and angled his body to make it less of a target. As he prepared to draw his pistol and confront whoever it was in the darkness, a male voice suddenly called out: "Hello by the fire! May we come on?"

"You may," Wyatt replied, "but do it slow and easy, if you please."

"We're on foot," the man said. "There's just the three of us and our horses."

After a moment three figures emerged into the firelight. Wyatt could see the shadows of their mounts behind them in the darkness.

"You're Wyatt Earp?" one of the men said, and Wyatt nodded.

Two of the men were dressed in the dark blue uniforms of the Army cavalry. The one who had spoken was a Lieutenant and white; the second man was Mexican, and by the look of his insignia, a Cavalryman.

The third, however, was dressed in plain frontier clothing and was taller than either of the soldiers. He was clearly Apache, but Wyatt, much like any lawmen of the time, would have recognized him anywhere. That strong, wide face had been staring out of wanted posters from the northern territories to south of the border for more than twenty years.

"Da go Ya, Goyathlay," Wyatt said in Apache. "Greetings, One Who Yawns."

The leathery-skinned Indian stared at him without replying, his expression neutral. The Lieutenant pointed at the ground by the fire. "Sit," he ordered.

Without taking his eyes off of Wyatt, Geronimo sank gracefully down into a cross-legged position with both hands resting on his knees.

"You men want some coffee?" Wyatt asked the two soldiers. They shook their heads and remained standing.

"No, thank you, sir," said the Lieutenant. "We're only here to escort *him.*"

The last word was loaded with a barely contained mix of hatred and fear, the kind Wyatt had seen all too often during his many years in the west.

It wasn't just Army men or bounty hunters who held this deep hostility toward the Indians. More civilian settlers and more Mexicans than he cared to think about felt the same way ~ people who weren't soldiers or men of low character, but the kind who ran the mercantiles and who were judges or farmers or ranchers or any of a dozen other professions in the rapidly shrinking frontier. Of all the Indian tribes, it was perhaps the Apache who evoked the worst of this hostility, and none more so than Geronimo. His name meant 'he who yawns', that was true enough; but there was nothing at all sedentary about the legendary raider,

By all accounts he was fifty, maybe sixty, but the truth is, no one really knew for sure how old he was. His frame, although stocky, was clearly still flexible and lithe; and even though his hair had grayed and his skin was as dark and wrinkled as old buffalo hide, his flint-colored eyes were still bright and aware. His gaze was that of a brave two-thirds his age, and to Wyatt's practiced eye he appeared as tense—and as dangerous — as a coiled wagon spring.

"You're not planning to stay until morning?" Wyatt asked.

The Mexican soldier shook his head. "No, señor, we ride for Fort Apache tonight. Unless you need for us to stay." He glanced down meaningfully at Geronimo.

"I'm sure I'll make do just fine," Wyatt said. "He armed?"

Grinning, the Lieutenant said, "No, sir. We're not that stupid. Meaning no disrespect, Mr. Earp, sir."

"I suspect not," Wyatt said. Still, he'd seen men do much dumber things. In the past, assuming had made an ass out of smarter men than him and he'd learned the hard way that it never hurt to check your proverbial saddle so that you didn't fall on what sat in it.

"Will that be all, sir?" the Lieutenant said.

Clearly, the two soldiers were ready to leave. It was a long ride back to Fort Apache and Wyatt could think of no reason to keep them any longer. "That'll be all," he replied. "Thank you for the help, gentlemen."

The Lieutenant saluted and then hesitated for a moment before staring down at Geronimo. "May I speak frankly, sir?"

Wyatt nodded.

"If he gives you any trouble, shoot him. You don't and he'll slit your throat the first chance he gets."

"That'll be enough," Wyatt snapped, suddenly tired of the white Lieutenant's obvious prejudice. "This man is a leader of his people and you'll treat him as one."

The Lieutenant's eyes widened for a moment, then narrowed in anger. He looked as if he were about to say something rash. Clearly, however, the look on Wyatt's face dissuaded him from starting something he instinctively knew he couldn't finish.

Instead, the Lieutenant simply nodded, then spun on his heel and strode into the darkness. The Mexican Cavalryman looked at Wyatt, a curious expression on his face, and then followed after his superior.

After they well away and the sound of them had been swallowed by the desert, Wyatt glanced over at

Geronimo. The Apache hadn't moved during his exchange with the two soldiers. "I'm going to put out this fire," Wyatt said carefully in English. "Then we're going to move down into the canyon for the night. Are you and me going to have a problem, Goyathlay?"

Wyatt pushed himself up onto his left knee and began breaking up the fire with a stick, careful to keep his eyes on the silent Apache.

When Geronimo still did not respond, Wyatt said, "If you're going to stay quiet, I'm going to get mighty

nervous. If I'm nervous, that means I might have to tie you up for my peace of mind. So what's it going to be? Trussed up like a hog or walking upright like a man?"

For a moment, Wyatt imagined he saw a twitch start below Geronimo's left eye. Then the Apache nodded slowly.

"You have honored me with my given name, Wyatt Earp," he said in English. "Why did you do that?" His voice, to Wyatt's surprise, was deep and rich and his pronunciation was as precise as an educated man's.

"Seemed polite," Wyatt replied, then went back to breaking up the fire.

Geronimo watched him for a moment, and then said, "I know of you, Wyatt Earp. Why did you bring me here? I have been at peace on San Carlos with my people for a long time."

"Not all that long," Wyatt observed. "Two years ago you were raiding settlements and hiding down Mexico way."

Before Geronimo could respond, Wyatt held up his hand. "Which isn't here nor there, far as I'm concerned. All I care about now is why you're here tonight."

"I am here," Geronimo said, sounding slightly annoyed, "because Colonel Joe said I must."

"Colonel Joe?" Wyatt raised one eyebrow.

"He is, as your people say, 'in charge,'" Geronimo said.

"I see." Wyatt finished tamping out the fire and then scattered dirt over the last of the warm embers. He gathered up his bedroll and Geronimo rose to his feet along with him.

"I still wish to know why *you* have brought me here," Geronimo said.

"That," Wyatt replied, tucking his bedroll under his arm, "will take some explaining, and I'll get to it soon enough. In the meantime, I know you're an honorable man, Goyathlay. So I'll take you at your word if you say we can bunk down tonight and I won't have to shoot you trying to escape."

Geronimo snorted derisively. "Escape, Wyatt Earp? Where would I go? My wife and my people are still prisoners of your Army."

He had a point, Wyatt realized. The old Apache was no longer the wild young brave who had roamed the western frontier with near impunity, hunted by the Army and renowned as a near-supernatural figure impervious even to bullets. Now he was just a man, growing older as they all were, and apparently wanting nothing more than to live with his family in peace.

It was a sentiment that, in many ways, Wyatt could relate to and he felt a stab of sympathy for the old Apache. "Just call me Wyatt," he said gruffly and strode over to his horse.

As he threw on his saddle and cinched it into place, Geronimo fetched his own horse and walked over with the animal in tow. "I will call you just Wyatt," he said, "and you will call me just Geronimo. That is what I am known as by the Mexicans and by many of your people, and it will suffice."

They both climbed onto their horses.

So *now* you must tell me," Geronimo continued as they rode away from the campsite, "why did you bring me here, Wyatt?"

"Like I said," Wyatt replied, "it's a long story, one that started with a letter. But that's mostly the now of it. The then of it goes back a whole lot further..."

T he rest of the night passed uneventfully. By the time dawn had broken over the desert and the coal black of night had been supplanted by the ash gray light of the rising sun, Wyatt and Geronimo were already up and preparing for the long ride ahead. Following a breakfast of bread and beans washed down with coffee brewed from the previous night's grounds, they mounted up and headed north.

By the time the sun had fully risen over the horizon, bringing the temperature up a full twenty degrees in less than an hour, the two of them were already several miles from their campsite. Wyatt had already begun to perspire and he knew from past experience that it would only get worse as the day wore on.

After riding for a while in silence, Geronimo said, "I have been thinking about what you have told me, Wyatt, and still I do not understand much of it."

"Is that so," Wyatt said, wiping away a line of sweat from beneath the brim of his hat.

"Yes. This priest has no hold over you, yet you claim a debt to him which does not exist."

"That's where you're wrong," Wyatt said. "There are three kinds of debts in this world, Geronimo: one

that a man signs his name to; one that comes from honor and keeping your word; and every so often, one that a man has to pay to himself, to make something right that he knows is wrong. You follow?"

Geronimo allowed himself the slightest of smiles. "Honor is something my people understand," he said. "It is the white man who often fails to keep his word."

Wyatt shrugged. "I can't argue that," he said. "Your people haven't gotten a fair shake over much of anything."

They continued in silence for a while. Then Geronimo said, "Still, I do not see how you are in debt to this priest. Already you had killed the outlaw named Waite, which is what the priest wanted from you in the first place."

"I'm no assassin," Wyatt snapped, "and don't you think for a second that I am. That son-of-a-bitch was killing the Indians in Pedro's care and scalping them for the bounty. Some of 'em were just kids. He drew down on me and I had no choice but to shoot him."

"But then your Father Pedro repaid his debt to you by shooting the man who—"

"Listen," Wyatt interrupted, "he is not *my* Father Pedro; the man's a damned troublemaker in more ways than I care to talk about. I'd have never come across Jesse Waite, or be on this damned fool ride, if it weren't for him. Second of all, I can see where you're going with this and it isn't as simple as you're making it out to be."

Before Geronimo could reply, the Apache sat up in his saddle and cocked his head, listening intently. Then he stared at two towering mesas which rose up from the desert several miles ahead. The trail they were on went straight through the middle of the twin monoliths, undoubtedly following a long and twisting canyon which extended all the way to the opposite side.

"There are rifles being fired," Geronimo said solemnly, pointing toward the mesas. "Can you not hear them, Wyatt?"

Wyatt grimaced. "Damn it, Geronimo, I wish you hadn't said that. We don't have time to get involved in a gunfight."

The trail they were riding clearly led toward whatever conflict was taking place inside the canyon. Wyatt knew that if they were going to get past the mesas in a reasonable time, then they had no choice but to proceed -- and to deal with whatever trouble awaited them there. What he *didn't* say was that there was more than lost time at stake. They might be riding into a simple robbery gone wrong, or it could be something worse -- like a band of Apache, for example.

If it turned out to be the latter Wyatt knew he could find himself in a mighty tight spot, especially with Geronimo along.

Given the choice, he thought wryly, he would have preferred a gang of rustlers shooting out their differences rather than a bunch of Apache.

Geronimo seemed to sense the direction of Wyatt's thinking, for he said, "If this is an attack by my

people I may be able to stop it, even if it is only long enough for us to pass."

"You'd do that?" Wyatt asked, glancing over at him.

"If what you have told me is true," Geronimo replied, "then we must hurry to help this Father Pedro. I have given my word to you and this I will do."

"Even if it's Apaches or another tribe you've made war with?" Wyatt pressed.

"Yes," Geronimo nodded. "It does not matter who they are. I will force them to let us pass."

Wyatt chewed his lip for a moment, considering his options. In truth, there really weren't any. Riding around the mesas would take the better part of a day, if not longer. On the other hand, if they rode into a gun fight, it had the potential to turn into a long, drawn-out standoff which might see them pinned down for more than a day. That said, one scenario was a certainty. The other was anything but.

When you got right down to it, Wyatt realized, there really wasn't any choice at all. "The hell with it," he said, digging in his heels. "Let's ride."

Both men spurred their horses across the open desert at full gallop.

A plume of dust rose up and hung in the hot, still air of their wake. Wyatt knew that if there were any lookouts near the mouth of the canyon, then their aggressive approach had erased any element of surprise. He pushed his horse harder, hoping the increased speed would give the men in the canyon less time to prepare for their arrival.

As they approached the canyon entrance, Wyatt drew his Army Colt and both men slowed their horses to a canter. The passage into the canyon was narrow and bordered on both sides by tumbled rocks of various sizes and shapes. There were more than enough places for one or more men to hide and Wyatt fully expected to hear a shout of alarm or to be fired upon.

But nothing happened.

The only sounds were the labored breathing of their horses and the muffled sounds of gunfire emanating from far inside the canyon. After a moment, Wyatt holstered his pistol and looked over at Geronimo. "What do you figure?" he said.

"There are many rifles," Geronimo replied after listening for a bit, "and pistols, too. Perhaps ten or twelve at most."

"That's a hell of a lot of shooting," Wyatt commented thoughtfully.

Once again, he considered riding around the mesas and avoiding the whole mess altogether, then rejected the idea almost as fast as it had come. He had urgent business with Father Pedro. The quicker it was over, the sooner he could get back to his life, even if that meant they had to ride through this canyon come hell or high water.

"All right, then," Wyatt said. "Let's get this done."

They entered the canyon side by side. The sheer rock walls towered over the trail, reminding Wyatt more than a little of prison walls. He knew that if things went badly the canyon could easily become a prison from which there would be no escape.

The further in they went, the more the trail began to turn and twist. Sometimes it became so narrow that they were forced to ride through a passage, one in front of the other, their knees brushing against the rock as they passed.

By now, the sound of the gunfire had grown louder, reverberating off the rock and making it impossible to tell how far away they were from the actual battle. The echoes would mask the sound of their approach, though, an advantage Wyatt was more than happy to take.

Just when he was beginning to think the gunfight might not be taking place in the canyon at all, they rode around a curve in the trail and found themselves in a wide open wash bathed in the clean, white light of the mid-morning sun.

A solitary wagon was pulled up against the canyon wall a dozen yards to their left. Wyatt could see a woman crouched inside the bed, a .40 caliber Marlin rifle propped over the rear gate. She was firing off to their right, where a number of Indians and a couple of Mexicans were crouched behind a grouping of large boulders with their left flank exposed to Wyatt and Geronimo's position.

The woman wasn't alone. A man lay partially concealed behind a line of smaller rocks in front of the wagon, firing a Sharps carbine toward their attackers. From what Wyatt could see the two of them were in the much weaker position, and as a result weren't inflicting much damage on their assailants.

When Wyatt and Geronimo reigned in their horses, everyone stopped firing and stared at them in surprise. The echoes of gunfire faded away, and a pall of acrid black powder smoke clouded the air. He and Geronimo looked at each other for a moment and then, almost as one, threw themselves from their horses.

The attackers scrambled around the rocks until they were no longer exposed, splitting half of their fire toward Wyatt and Geronimo. Wyatt stayed in the open just long enough to yank his rifle and an extra pistol out of his saddle before diving for cover as bullets kicked up the soft sand around his feet.

He saw Geronimo roll behind a boulder and threw him the extra pistol, hoping he wasn't making a fatal

mistake entrusting the Apache with a loaded weapon.

The Lieutenant had said they weren't stupid enough to arm Geronimo, Wyatt thought with amusement, yet here he was doing just that. He sincerely hoped he lived long enough to appreciate the irony of his actions.

Geronimo leaned around his boulder and fired once before ducking back down. Wyatt looked over just in time to see one of the Indians drop his rifle and pitch over backward out of sight.

Wyatt took aim at one of the Mexicans peering around a rock, then fired three times in rapid succession. The first two shots went wild, sending rock chips flying into the air, but the third one found its mark. The Mexican slumped over sideways, blood turning the sand ruby red beneath him.

Crawling on his hands and knees, Wyatt moved behind a smaller boulder and fired again. One of the

Indians shot back and he felt the air from the bullet's passage against his cheek. Irritated, he fired again. The Indian screamed in pain and clutched his shoulder. Before Wyatt could finish him, someone pulled the injured man out of sight.

"You're outnumbered!" Wyatt hollered toward the attackers. "We're not alone and there's a whole regiment riding behind us! Throw down your guns and you won't be hurt!"

"The hell you say, señor!" one of the Mexicans screamed.

'Give it up now!' Wyatt shouted, but he knew his threat had no teeth. The men had probably gotten a clear look at Geronimo. That, along with the fact that neither of them was wearing an Army uniform, stripped away whatever credibility his threat might have held. Still, they were causing damage, probably more then the attackers had expected when they took on the two people in the wagon.

If Wyatt had his way, they'd do a lot more damage before the day was done.

Drawing his second pistol, he waited for a lull in the gunfire. Then he rose up on both knees, firing both Colts in unison. He caught a Mexican and an Indiana partially exposed but missed them both. When they saw Wyatt they immediately began shooting in his direction. None of their shots found their mark, but a shard of rock from the boulder nicked his cheek causing a narrow ribbon of blood to run down the side of his face.

Throwing himself down in the sand, Wyatt used his elbows to pull himself along on his chest, maneuvering until he could see the wagon. The man lying in front of it was pinned down. Then, inexplicably, he tried to stand, probably to take cover inside, and that was his undoing.

A bullet caught him in the side and spun him around, knocking the Sharps rifle out of his hands. He staggered away from the wagon and into the open, badly wounded and disoriented. Wyatt exhaled sharply, fully expecting him to be riddled with bullets.

But that didn't happen.

Instead, the attackers intensified their assault, forcing Wyatt to hunker down behind the boulder as rock chips and dust filled the air over his head. Just before he hit the ground, Wyatt saw the woman in the wagon fall back out of sight but couldn't tell if she'd been killed or only wounded. After a few minutes the gunfire stopped and silence once more reigned over the canyon. Wyatt reloaded his pistols, waiting for the bullets to start flying again.

They never did.

Finally, he emerged into the open, his Army Colts cocked and ready. However, Wyatt could hear the sounds of their horses retreating further into the canyon, and it was immediately obvious that the attackers had fled. It seemed they had come prepared for a hasty departure in case things didn't go their way. To his surprise, Wyatt saw that the injured man was gone. Clearly, he had been carried off by his assailants.

Strange behavior, Wyatt thought, for a bunch of ordinary bushwhackers.

He called out, "Hello in the wagon! Are you shot?"

There was no response. Wyatt moved forward cautiously and Geronimo joined him, moving with great stealth in case any of the attackers had remained behind to ambush them. However, it appeared that all of them were gone, leaving only their dead behind.

Approaching the rear of the wagon, Wyatt called out again, "I'm coming inside. We're friends, so don't fire!"

boards, her eyes closed. She was a tiny little thing, Wyatt noted with amazement, barely five foot tall and no more than a hundred pounds. A bullet had creased her forehead, apparently knocking her unconscious, but other than that she appeared unharmed. Wyatt holstered his pistols and climbed into the wagon.

As he bent over her, he heard the sound of a pistol being cocked just inches from his ear. He froze as the

bitter end of the barrel came up against his temple. Looking down, Wyatt found himself staring into gray eyes as cold and clear as a mountain stream.

"If you're a friend," she said, "then you won't mind moving real slow. Otherwise, I might turn out to be the worst one you ever met."

"You can rest easy," Wyatt said carefully. "We're here to help. My name's Earp. Wyatt Earp."

"Well, it's right nice to meet you," she said, "assuming that's your real name. The only Wyatt Earp I know of is Sheriff of Dodge City, Kansas, and that's awfully far from New Mexico."

"That may be," he said, "but I'm Wyatt just the same. And who might you be?"

She stared into his eyes for a moment as if trying to judge the truth by what she saw there. Finally she sighed and lowered the pistol, easing the hammer back into place. Wyatt exhaled sharply, rocking back on his heels. Geronimo came around the back of the wagon and stared impassively at both of them.

"My name's Annie," she said, wincing as she reached up and touched the cut on her forehead, "Annie Oakley." She nodded toward Geronimo. "Who's the Indian?"

"My name is Geronimo," he said before Wyatt could answer.

Annie stared at him for a moment, then burst out laughing.

"Of course you are," she said, wiping a tear from the corner of her eye. "Who else would you be?"

Wyatt failed to see what was so funny. They'd both risked their lives to help her; being laughed at seemed like piss-poor thanks for their trouble. "When you're through laughing," he said irritably, "those men took away the shooter out front."

"What?" Annie stopped laughing and sat up suddenly, then groaned and sank back down against the floorboards.

Take it easy," Wyatt said, suddenly sorry that he had been so blunt. "You got hit in the head pretty good. We need to get you patched up before you go riding off."

"You don't understand," she said, struggling to get up again. "That was my husband, Frank, and I've got to go after him."

"The men who shot him have gone," Geronimo said, "and besides, you cannot fight them alone."

"He's right," Wyatt said. "You're in no condition to ride anywhere right now. We have got to treat that head wound and get our bearings before we ride off half-cocked."

She looked like she wanted to argue some more, then finally nodded her assent.

"I'll fix her up," Wyatt told Geronimo. "You take a look at things out there and then we'll figure out our next step."

Geronimo nodded silently and moved off. Wyatt didn't bother to ask for his pistol back. Geronimo had already proven he could be trusted and he was pretty sure the Apache was going to need it again before this ride was over.

"Come on, then," Wyatt said, helping Annie out of the wagon. "Let's see to that cut."

For the next few hours Wyatt and Geronimo kept busy, fetching their horses, packing up Annie's gear, and checking the bodies of the fallen men, searching for clues as to where they had come from and why they had attacked the two travelers.

"Wyatt," Geronimo said, later that afternoon, "you must see this."

He had dragged two bodies out into the open, stretching them out side by side like slabs of beef. One of them was Mexican and the other an Indian. Geronimo had cut open the arms of their long-sleeved

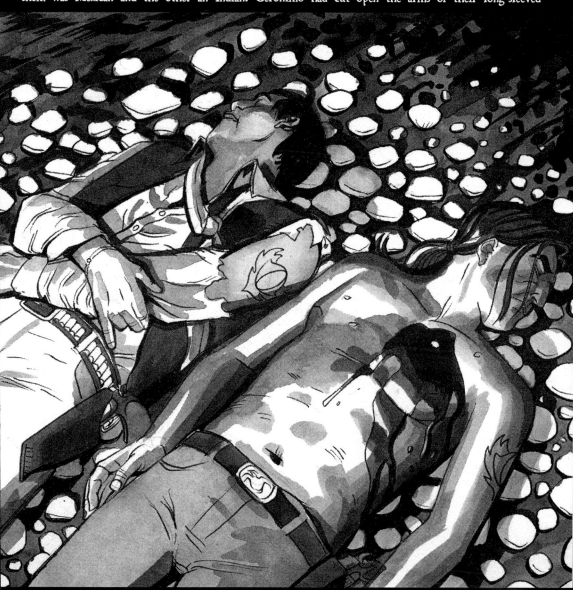

undershirts, revealing identical, detailed tattoos on the left biceps of both men.

When he saw the matching marks, Wyatt's breath caught in his throat. It was a design he knew well.

Fishing the priest's letter from his back pocket, he unfolded it and knelt down beside the Mexican's body. He held the paper beside the man's arm in order to compare the elaborate tattoo with the crude drawing on the back page of the letter.

The actual tattoo was far more elaborate than he would have imagined — an oval-shaped eye, similar to a cat's, but flared upward at both ends and surrounded by licks of blue-tinged flame. The pupil of the eye, and the flames which surrounded it, were so realistically rendered that they could only be the work of a master artisan.

Sighing, Wyatt stood up and refolded the paper - which was beginning to fray and separate along the folds - before shoving it into his back pocket. "That damned priest," he said irritably, "is going to get us all killed before this is done."

He jerked his head toward the fire, where Annie was reclining against her bedroll with a warm cloth pressed against her head wound. "Let's mount up," he said, "her included. We need to get on the trail now. If we're lucky, we'll catch up to those bastards before they can warn anyone else."

Geronimo nodded, studying Wyatt's face. "How many men await us where we are going, Wyatt? You have not yet told me our destination."

"And there's a damned good reason *why* I haven't told you," Wyatt snapped. "I don't know myself, for sure. Until I do, I'm keeping it to myself."

"As you wish." Geronimo nodded stiffly and turned back to his horse.

In truth, Wyatt wasn't sure why he still refused to tell the Apache everything contained in the priest's letter. What the hell difference did it make? Maybe he didn't want to believe all of it, not yet. Or maybe there was some other reason. He sighed. It didn't really matter, when you got right down to it. He still had to see this thing through. Perhaps with the help of a renegade Indian and a petite sharpshooter, it might just be enough.

"I'll tell you where we're going, Goyathlay," he said, more to himself than to anyone. "Straight to Hell, and in a handbasket to boot."

Geronimo turned to face him, one hand resting on the edge of his saddle. "Hell is a white man's place, Wyatt Earp," he said with a shrug. "I do not fear what I do not believe."

Wyatt glanced over at Annie. "You may not believe in it," he said, "but she surely does. And no one should ride into Hell without knowing what's ahead of 'em. I'm also not too inclined to take a woman into

a fight that ain't hers."

Frowning, Geronimo considered Wyatt's words. "When my people are attacked," he said finally, "all fight side by side, man and woman." He nodded toward Annie. "Her husband has been taken. This is her fight as well as ours."

Wyatt wanted to say 'It's really my fight and I haven't got around to telling you that just yet.' What he actually said was, "Fine. But she ain't gonna like what I've got to say."

"Good news travels on gentle winds, Wyatt," Geronimo said evenly, "but bad news rides upon the storm. This woman, like all of us, has known the lightning and the rain. She will understand."

Wyatt frowned. "I hope you're right," he said as they both walked toward the fire.

When Annie saw them approaching, she sat up and folded the damp cloth into quarters before setting it down carefully on the folds of her wool skirt. "Did you find out anything from those S.O.B.s?" she inquired archly.

"I'm afraid so," Wyatt said, sitting down on a flat rock beside the fire pit. He took a deep breath. "Those men who took your husband are part of something bigger, Ms. Oakley. I suspect their attack on you was about more than a simple trail robbery."

Annie sat up straighter and stared into Wyatt's eyes. "Sounds to me like you know something about all

this," she said, her voice hardening. "Did you have something to do with what happened here today, Mr. Earp?"

Wyatt took a deep breath to reign in the angry retort he'd been about to deliver. Something about Annie Oakley was like having a bur under his saddle. He suspected it was probably because she was more outspoken than most of the women he knew. Still, it was something he could get used to, given enough time. That was something he'd have to think on when this was all over ~ preferably with a cup of black coffee on the bar in front of him. Regrettably, especially at times like this, he no longer drank.

"Me knowing about it don't exactly mean I'm involved," he said, and immediately hated the defensive tone of his voice.

She raised her eyebrows at him but didn't speak.

"What I meant to say," he continued, flustered in spite of himself, "is that Geronimo and me are headed into some trouble and those fellas were involved. You come along and it'll be your trouble, too, Ms. Oakley."

"How so?" Annie asked, and then Wyatt saw terror flood her face. "Is my Frank dead, Mr. Earp?"

"Don't jump to conclusions now," Wyatt said quickly. "Your husband was shot up bad, but they still took him, which probably means he isn't dead. Not yet, anyway. The faster we mount up and head after them, the

better his chances are."

Annie pushed herself to her feet and stood there for a moment, swaying unsteadily. Wyatt and Geronimo both reached out to help her, but she waved them off.

"I agree with you, Mr. Earp," she said stiffly. "We ride now, no more waitin'."

"If you're sure—" Wyatt began, but Annie cut him off with a stern look.

"I said we ride," she said, "so let's not waste any more time jawin' about it. I'll not let those yellow cowards carry off my husband while I sit here feeling sorry for myself!"

"All right," Wyatt said, nodding his acquiescence. "It's decided, then."

"This will be a glorious battle," Geronimo said somberly. "Should we face death, then we do so as warriors. I am prepared."

You can go ahead and be prepared for the both of us, far as I'm concerned," Wyatt said, irritated. "Me, I'll hold off on my preparin' for a bit if it's all the same to you."

"But if it is our destiny to die in battle -" Geronimo said, but Wyatt shook his head angrily.

"Enough of that," he cut in. "I don't want to hear any more talk about death, understand? I'm in no hurry to visit the happy hunting ground, even if you are."

Geronimo shrugged noncommittally, leaving Wyatt to finish loading his horse in silence. When they

were finally done and Annie had secured her wagon as best she could, they all mounted up and rode out of the canyon together, following the trail of attacker's hoof prints into the open desert.

After riding for more than an hour, Wyatt felt the slightest stir of a breeze on his face. He knew that this usually meant heavy winds—and probably bad weather -- were not far behind. A storm, and especially the winds that preceded it, would wipe out much of the attacker's trail. Finding them when it was all over would be that much more difficult.

From the looks on their faces, Annie and Geronimo were both thinking the same thing. Pointing toward a rocky hill which protruded from the desert sand, Wyatt said, "We've got to make it to more solid ground before this storm picks up."

"Agreed," Geronimo said, "I will find the marks from their horses there. If the storm comes and their trail is lost, it will help me to find them again when the rain has passed.

As one, they broke into a gallop. As they crested the low hill, all three pulled back on their reins simultaneously and brought their mounts to an abrupt halt.

"Well I'll be damned," Annie said in wonder, staring at the desert floor on the other side of the hill. "You don't see that every day do you, Mr. Earp?"

"Perhaps it is a spirit," Geronimo said ominously, "sent here to warn us of our deaths."

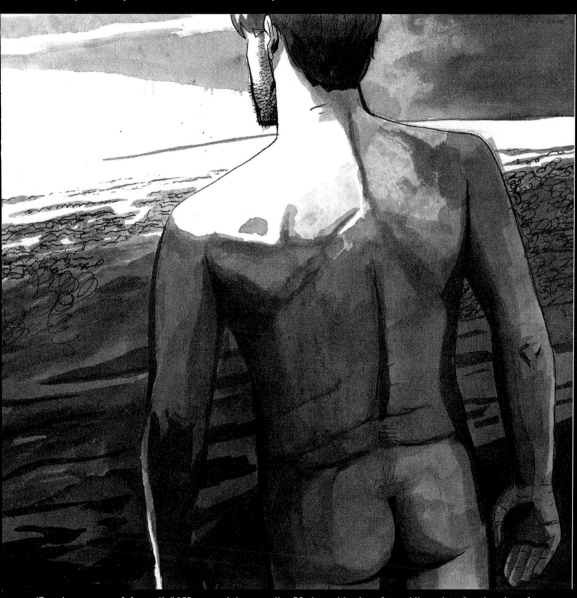

"I said, no more of that talk," Wyatt said distractedly. He leaned back in his saddle and took a deep breath. He'd seen a lot of things in his time: a man buried up to his neck by Indians, waiting with terror-filled eyes as a colony of fire ants climbed toward his face. Even a newfangled riding machine with a big wheel in front and a little one in back that you used your feet to move.

This, however, was something different. And then some.

During his twenty-five plus years in the desert and mountains, Wyatt had yet to see a naked man in the middle of nowhere, strolling along just as calmly as could be ~ oblivious to the sun and the heat and the fact that his pecker was swinging back and forth in front of God and all creation.

"He's no spirit, Geronimo," Wyatt said, "although there are probably a few men who'd call that naked butt of his a nightmare."

The stranger looked up in surprise at the sound of her voice. Seeing them astride their horses, the man yelled back, "You motherfuckers gonna come down here and lend me a hand? Or are you gonna just sit there,

watching me like some New York stage show?"

The sand had to be hotter than a cast iron stove at chowtime, Wyatt thought as he edged his horse down the side of the hill, but you'd never know it from the calm expression on the man's face.

"You've got a hell of a mouth on you," Wyatt said as he pulled up in front of him. "Far as I'm concerned, we could just as easily leave you walking until your feet burn off."

The man glared up at Wyatt, shielding his eyes from the sun and making no attempt to hide his nakedness. If that's the way you want to play it," he said. "You can help out or not, either way's the same to me.

"You really are a piece of work," Annie said, reining her horse up beside Wyatt's. "You'll die if we don't help you, mister. The least you could do is show a little bit of gratitude."

"Well, well," the man said, looking Annie up and down with an appreciate eye. "Ain't you a pretty one

if I do say so myself."

"She's a married woman, stranger," Wyatt said before Annie could respond, "and I'm mighty serious when I say your mouth is about to cost you plenty."

To Wyatt's astonishment the stranger laughed raucously, but only for a moment. When he stopped his lips hardened into a line, and Wyatt found himself staring into eyes as dark and inscrutable as a grizzly bear's.

"I'll tell you what," the stranger said softly. "You come down off that horse and we'll see who's the one walking and who's the one wearing the clothes, friend."

Wyatt immediately tensed and took a closer look at the stranger's face. It wasn't one he recognized from the many wanted posters that had come through his office in Dodge City, yet there was still something vaguely familiar about him. Nonetheless, he recognized the man for what he was: a gunfighter and one clearly not prone to idle threats.

"What's your name, stranger?" Wyatt asked, resting a hand on his Colt.

If the man noticed Wyatt's movement he made no sign of it. Instead, he just grinned. "The name's Thompson," he said, "but people call me The Cisco Kid."

"Hell, ma'am," Cisco said affably, "it's probably thirty-five or more. Just goes to show that you can't believe everything you hear. And what's your name, if you don't mind me being forward and all?"

"Annie," she said. "Annie Oakley." She pointed to her traveling companions and said, "This here's Wyatt Earp, and the Indian's the Apache they call Geronimo."

The Cisco Kid looked at each of them in silence. Then he said, "Glad to meet y'all. Now who's got a shirt and pants and a spot on their horse for me?"

After finding some clothes for Cisco and putting him double up with Geronimo, the four of them rode hard for another three hours, finally locating a much smaller mesa with a shallow cave to help shield them from the worst of the approaching storm.

While setting up camp they spotted a band of wild horses in the distance. After they had situated themselves, Geronimo and Cisco set out to capture one of the stallions for the latter's use the next day.

As darkness fell once more across the desert, and the light of the fire cast a comforting glow against the cave walls, Wyatt found himself relaxing a bit for the first time in what felt like years.

He and Annie sat in silence for a good while, each of them sipping black coffee as they watched the sparks somersault away from the flames on the strengthening breeze. The only sounds were the crackle of the burning wood and the occasional coyote somewhere in the onyx-black desert. After a while, Annie said, "You haven't told Geronimo, or any of us for that matter, the whole truth, have you?"

Wyatt didn't reply for a bit, and then he said, "Isn't much truth to tell, not yet anyway."

"With all due respect," Annie replied, "that is certainly a load of bull, Mr. Earp, and I think you know it."

He looked up expecting to see anger on her face, but all he saw was concern. Surprised, he said, "If this is about your husband   "

She shook her head. "It isn't about Frank, not entirely. This is about *all* of us. Truth be told, it was

Geronimo that got me to thinking - and let me tell you, I've been doing a plumb lot of that since you two came upon us in that canyon."

"Geronimo's in my custody," Wyatt said, annoyed by her inquisitive tone. "It isn't like he's running around a free man."

"Oh, I don't doubt he's in your custody," Annie said, "although it does seem a bit risky for him to have a pistol."

Wyatt winced involuntarily.

Still, I wondered why you had him along, since last I heard, he was an Army prisoner. Of course, I haven't yet gotten a straight answer to most of my questions, that being just one of them. I'm presuming you could clear up quite a few of them if you were of a mind to."

"You presume a lot," Wyatt said, pushing himself up to a sitting position and tossing the lukewarm contents of his cup into some nearby sage. "What makes you think I've got any answers at all?"

"That's easy," she said, leaning forward and staring him in the eye. "We're all riding toward the same place, and somehow, you're in the middle of the whole thing, Mr. Earp. I caught me a glimpse of that letter you're carrying in your pocket and I do believe that piece of paper makes you the answer man."

Before Wyatt could retort, he heard the sound of horses approaching the camp. Glancing at Annie, he said, "We'll talk more about this."

Both of them stood up as Geronimo rode into the firelight. Beside him, the Cisco Kid sat astride a handsome mustang complete with a saddle and bedroll. There was even the butt of a Winchester sticking out of an elaborate saddle scabbard.

At Wyatt's questioning expression, Cisco said, "When we got up to the herd, we found this one amongst them. Geronimo here figures it came from one of those fellas you all shot."

"That is not all," Geronimo said, pointing at the scabbard's fancy tooling.

Walking over to the horse, Wyatt leaned over and took a closer look at the weapon, petting the horse's muzzle as he did so. There, carefully worked into the leather, was another image of the tattoo.

"But this ain't the best part," Cisco said. "We found ourselves a lot more than a horse and rig."

Wyatt glanced past him, and that's when he saw the woman on the horse. She had stayed back out of the firelight, silently observing their exchange. She was what you might call handsome, more ordinary than beautiful -- what Wyatt's mother would have called "rough around the edges" -- and her deeply tanned skin bespoke of much time spent exposed to the elements. Wyatt was also sure she'd seen more than her fair share of trouble.

His years of experience as a peace officer had left him with a strange instinct for these matters which was rarely proven wrong.

"Come on and join us," Wyatt said cautiously, and she did, tying off her horse beside theirs and then joining them by the fire.

"My name is Belle," she said, once they were all seated and sipping fresh coffee. "I've been riding for the past two days, since me and my husband, Sam, were attacked."

"Where's your husband now?"

"The penes took him," she said, her voice dripping with disgust. "I don't know where they went but I aim to get him back."

"It happened just the same way with Annie here," Cisco said. "What do you make of that, Wyatt?"

"I'll be more inclined to let you know," Wyatt said, "if you kindly shut the hell up and let her finish her story."

Cisco's eyes narrowed in anger, but when he saw the expression on Wyatt's face, he scowled and stared into the fire.

"Go on," Wyatt said, nodding at Belle. "Tell the rest of it."

We were makin' our way toward Indian Territory when a band of Inch came up on us," she continued. "At first, they pretended to be friendly, but Sam knew different. They took our wagon and my Sam, too, but they left me with a horse." She grimaced. "They said they didn't want to leave a woman to die in the desert."

"Yet they did not leave her water," added Geronimo somberly. "They had to know this would mean her death."

"These boys are real bastards," Wyatt said thoughtfully, "and apparently, they aren't above killing men, women, or even children if the mood strikes 'em."

What Wyatt didn't say was that this kind of behavior was spelled out in the priest's letter. It was getting high time to reveal everything he knew, but he needed just a little more corroboration before telling them the whole story.

"They do seem like real assholes," Cisco said helpfully. "I'll be more'n happy to shoot some of them cocksuckers, especially the ones that left me in the desert. Just point me in the right direction."

"You're mighty quick to reach for a pistol," Wyatt said, "but in case it escaped your notice, we aren't an Army detachment. We find those boys, taking them on is going to take more than a handful of pistols and rifles."

"Well, unless you've got some riders of your own waiting to join us, I don't know how you plan to get anywhere near 'em without getting all of our heads blown off," Cisco replied.

"I'm still working on that," Wyatt said. "But that's for the morning. Tonight, we have to wait out this

storm. When the sun's up, we'll see if Geronimo can track them. Most of their prints will be gone, if not all of them, so he'll have his work cut out."

They all agreed that this was the best plan. Then Cisco asked, "So what's your story there, Belle?"

"What makes you think I have any kind of story?" she replied sullenly.

Now that they had been sitting in the firelight for a while and Wyatt had been able to study her face, something about it nagged at the back of his mind. Unlike the Cisco Kid, hers was a face that he most definitely recognized. However, for the life of him, he couldn't remember from where.

"Me, I'm just a simple cowboy," Cisco said amiably, "but I get the feeling you've seen more than your share of the train. Seems to me that would make for an interesting tale or two.

Belle looked at him for a moment and then burst out in raucous, booming laughter. Cisco looked disgruntled but did not respond. When she had finished laughing, she took a sip of her coffee and shook her head, still chuckling. "It seems to me you're full of shit there, Cisco, if you don't mind me a sayin' so."

"There seems to be a lot that going around tonight," Annie murmured, and Wyatt shot her a dirty look.

"What are you talking about, woman?" Cisco said, clearly uncomfortable.

"'Simple cowboy', hell," Belle snorted. "You surely are a killer for hire and a dangerous man, and don't you be pretendin' you're anything else."

"Funny thing is, this morning he was bragging that he'd killed more than thirty men," Annie said pleasantly. "I don't think he mentioned 'simple cowboy' as part of his description."

"That's *thirty-five* men," Cisco practically snarled at her, "probably more, but that ain't here nor there."

"No, it sure isn't," Wyatt interjected, "but here's what I think. Maybe you maybe killed that many men, Cisco, maybe not. If you did, it was probably justified, else I'd have seen your face on the wall of the sheriff's office before now." He nodded at Belle. "Now you, on the other hand, are something else entirely. I know your face from somewhere. Have we ever met before?"

Belle pursed her lips for a moment before replying. Then she drew herself up proudly and said, "We ain't ever met, Mr. Earp, but being a Marshall and all, you'd have heard of my Sam and me. We've been on the opposite side of the law a time or two. My full name's Starr, Belle Starr."

"Is that a fact," Wyatt said, his eyes narrowing.

Of course he'd heard of Sam Starr and his notorious gunslinging wife, Belle. They had been outlaws on and off, mostly down around Texas and Arkansas. It should have come to him right away, but the last thing he expected was to find her riding alone through the middle of New Mexico.

"I do know of you," he admitted. "I heard you used to run with Jesse James and the Youngers."

"Sure, when I was a young 'un," she said scornfully, "but we was all just kids back in them days. Course, I knew them a long time after that, too." She squared her shoulders and stared into Wyatt's eyes. "If you have a mind to take Sam and me in, Marshall Earp, you can forget about that. Right now we ain't wanted anywhere, and I plan to keep it that way."

"I'm no Marshall," Wyatt said, "at least, not at the moment. Right now I'm just a man paying off an old debt."

He may be paying off a debt," Annie said, "but I'm on this trail to get my husband back and nothing more."

"I am here because Colonel Joe -" Geronimo began, but Wyatt cut him off with a stare that could have melted sand.

"Well, speaking for me," Cisco said, "I'm just here to pay back the cocksuckers who left me to die. Earp here seems to know where to find 'em, and that's the long and short of it."

"From what I saw this morning," Annie said, "it's more the short of it than anything else."

Cisco's face turned scarlet. "Hey, now, that ain't hardly right, it was mighty hot out there!"

"A man's willy don't shrink in the heat," Belle said, glancing at Cisco, "only in the cold. Course, with *some* men it don't make no difference either way."

"I can't say I care one way or the other," Wyatt said gruffly to keep from laughing. "As it is, I've heard and seen enough of Cisco's prick for two lifetimes. Now why don't you all get some sleep? We've got a long ride ahead of us tomorrow."

As if on cue, thunder rumbled across the desert. On the horizon, lightning tore jagged tears across a sky blackened by coils of vicious looking storm clouds.

"Rain is coming," Geronimo said unnecessarily, and they were all silent, staring out at the distant tempest.

Wyatt tossed some more wood on the fire as a new gust of wind, stronger than before but with a bitterly cold edge, pushed at the dying flames as if trying to snuff them out.

Closing his eyes, Wyatt leaned back against the log and pulled his blanket up around his shoulders, hoping to get some rest before daylight came.

As was the way with some desert storms, the rain came hard and fast in the night, pounding the desert for a few hours before moving on.

When the first hints of sunlight finally peeked over the horizon, casting the desert in pale shades of black and gray, Wyatt rolled out of his blanket and stood up quietly so as not to wake the others. Moving carefully, he went to the mouth of the cave and stared out into the pre-dawn darkness.

He took a deep breath, enjoying the fresh, earthly smell of the air after a rainstorm. Then he walked quietly away from the smoldering fire and his sleeping companions, hoping to find some privacy so he could relieve himself.

Slipping behind a large boulder, he unbuttoned his pants and then his union suit and began to relieve himself. As he was finishing up, he heard the sound of gravel shifting behind him and froze.

"Don't move one fuckin' bit," said a low voice from just over his shoulder, "or I'll kill you where you stand."

Wyatt grimaced in disgust. His Colt was lying back by the fire, which didn't do him a damned bit of good standing there with his prick in his hand.

"I'm not moving," he said calmly, wanting very badly to put close himself back up, but sure that if he tried he'd get a bullet in the back for his trouble.

Wyatt had heard of poetic justice before. After making fun of Cisco's nakedness, he supposed this probably qualified.

"Ya'll were supposed to sleep till the sun come up," the voice said peevishly, and Wyatt suddenly realized that it belonged to a boy who was maybe as young as fifteen.

"If you're angling for a robbery," Wyatt said softly, "then you picked the wrong group. If I were you I'd just ride on while you can."

"I ain't no robber," the boy hissed. "I'm here for some respon   for some respon-damnit to hell!" The boy was clearly struggling with a word he'd never used before.

"Responsibility?" Wyatt offered.

"That's it," the boy said. "They trusted me, told me I was to come back here and plug y'all, and that's what I'm gonna do. Then, when I gets back, Kane is gonna know my name and I'm gonna be a big shot, sure as hell."

"Well, you pull that trigger and the others are going to hear it," Wyatt said. "I doubt you'll get very far."

"Nope," the boy said proudly, "that's why you and I are gonna just march over there together, then I'll put some lead in all five of 'ya at the same time. What do think of that, mister smart ass?"

"I think you talk too much," Wyatt said wearily. "And there's no way in hell I'm walking over there all unbuttoned like this. So either you let me put myself away or just go ahead and pull that trigger right now."

Wyatt could sense that the boy was struggling to process this ultimatum. Finally, he said, "All right, then, fix yourself up, old man. Then get to movin' so I can finish this."

Before Wyatt could take a step, however, another voice said, "For once I've gotta agree with Earp here ~ you *do* talk too much, boy."

Then Wyatt heard a loud thump and the boy cried out in pain. Turning, Wyatt saw the boy collapse face down in the sand, a bloody patch matting the hair on the back of his head. A surprisingly new and expensive pistol lay a few inches away from his outstretched and motionless fingers.

Cisco stepped out from behind the boulder, his gun held out butt-first. When Wyatt saw that the hammer of the boy's pistol was cocked, he realized that he had come perilously close to buying the farm. If it hadn't been for Cisco, he might well have. "Looks like I owe you one," he said, staring down at the

unconscious boy. "You suppose you killed him?"

Cisco shook his head. "Nah, didn't hit the little weasel hard enough. He'll have one hell of a headache when he wakes up, though."

"Let's get him over to the fire," Wyatt said. "We'll truss him up and throw some water in his face."

Wyatt picked the pistol up from the ground and uncocked the hammer before sticking it in his waistband. Then he grabbed the boy's arms while Cisco took his feet. Working together, they walked the inert body over to the fire and dropped it unceremoniously on the ground.

Geronimo, Annie, and Belle had been awakened by the commotion. They studied the unconscious boy with interest while Wyatt and Cisco tied him up. Annie had already stoked the buried coals and flames were licking hungrily at the pile of dry wood they'd kept out of the rain.

"Who is the hell is that?" Belle asked.

"That kid caught old Wyatt here with his pants down," Cisco said gleefully as they sat down by the fire. "Had the draw on him and everything. It was a real sight to see!"

"I'm glad you enjoyed yourself," Wyatt said. "Now tie the little bastard up and throw some water in his face. I've got a few questions for him." He glanced at Annie. "You wanted answers," he said, "now you're going

to get some."

It took a couple of tries before the boy started to come around. He was clearly in pain and furious upon realizing that he'd been caught and restrained. While Wyatt and the others calmly drank their morning coffee, he struggled mightily against the ropes. This went on for ten or fifteen minutes before he finally relented, his face shiny with the sweat of his exertions.

"So you finished with all that?" Wyatt asked calmly. "If you want to give it another try, we've got time."

"Fuck you," the boy said, "Kane's going to kill all of you, just wait and see."

"Perhaps so," Geronimo said, "but we all must die sooner or later. Even this man that you speak of."

"Kane'll never die," the boy insisted, staring at Wyatt with hate-filled eyes, "but you fuckers will for sure.

He'll roast you like pigs on a fuckin' stick."

"For a boy who probably hasn't done it before, you sure do like to say that foul word,'" Annie said.

"Whatever you say, bitch," the kid said, sneering. "You wanna know something else? Kane gets a look at you, he'll fuck you like the whore you are. And when he's done, he'll toss what's left of you into the Eye to rot along with the rest of the—"

The kid never got to finish his sentence. Moving faster than Wyatt would have believed possible, Annie

snatched up her Marlin rifle with one hand and fired from the waist, not bothering to sight along the barrel.

Screaming, the kid rolled onto his back, blood streaming from the side of his head where his left ear had been only a second before.

Wyatt noted with amazement that Annie was still holding her cup in her other hand. She lowered the rifle with practiced ease and resumed drinking her coffee as if nothing special had happened.

Geronimo, Cisco, and Bell were all staring at her in astonishment. Wyatt knew he probably had a similar expression on his own face. Cisco was the first to speak.

"Well, I'll be damned," he said admiringly. "That was something and a ham shank, too. If you weren't already hitched, Annie, I'd marry you myself."

Annie smiled demurely. "Why thank you, Cisco. That's awfully sweet of you to say. It wasn't anything but some trick shooting, the same kind me and Frank do all over the country."

"Call it whatever you want," Cisco said, clearly smitten, "it was still a thing of beauty, it truly was."

After a few minutes the kid's screams became hoarse, snot-filled sobs. The jagged wound where his ear had been was still bleeding freely, but none of them stood up to do anything about it.

Wyatt looked over at the boy, his face devoid of pity. He'd known more than a few like him over the years, youngsters with no conscience and no sense of right or wrong and tempers as volatile as a bottle of Swedish Blasting Oil. Mostly, they grew up to be killers or just bad men in general. In his experience, putting them down early on was usually better for everyone involved.

Even in his pain, the kid's hatred for them was palpable. Wyatt shook his head and said, "I'm guessing you'd be better off watching your tongue, least while you still have one.I suspect Annie here could shoot it clean out of your mouth if she was inclined to."

The kid worked his tongue around in his mouth, clearly unsure of what to say, keeping his eyes on Annie the entire time. Finally, he said, "If y'all know what's good for you, you'll untie me and head out of here. Kane'll be —"

"That man isn't going to do one damned thing for you," Wyatt interrupted. "So save your breath. You want to make it out of this alive, I'd stop running your goddamn trap and listen up. We understand each other?"

After considering Wyatt's words, the boy nodded his assent.

"Okay, then," Wyatt continued, "here's how this is going to work. I'm going to ask you some questions and you're gonna answer them, keeping the bullshit to a minimum. We clear?"

Annie reached down casually and stroked the barrel of her Marlin. The kid's eyes moved frantically back and forth between her and Wyatt, and then he nodded.

"Glad to hear it," Wyatt said. "First question: who's this Kane fella you've been jawing about?"

So the kid told them. That, and a lot more.

When he was done talking, Wyatt tossed a spare knife behind a nearby pile of rubble then propped the boy up by the fire so that he could free himself after they were gone. Before the group left, Cisco advised the boy to ride as far and as fast as he could in the opposite direction.

As they rode away they were silent, each of them lost in contemplation of everything the boy had told them.

Even as the first rays of the sun began to cut through the morning chill, it failed to dispel the cold resolve which now drove them toward their final destination — a dark and lonely place known as the Devil's Eye.

By the time night had fallen on the fourth day, Wyatt and the others had ridden for nearly twelve hours, stopping only twice to water their horses and rest before continuing on. When the temperature began to drop and the last rays of the sun had been consumed by darkness, they stopped for a third time to get their bearings and prepare for what was to come.

Because they were now so close to their objective and did not want to prematurely encounter a patrol, they refrained from setting a fire. Instead, they sat on their bedrolls in the dark to discuss their plan, such as it was.

"So you figure everything the kid said is true?" Cisco asked, sipping some water from his canteen. "I mean, hell, Wyatt, it's one thing to plug a couple of the cocksuckers but it's something else to take on an army."

Wyatt stroked his moustache for a bit, considering his reply. The truth of the matter was, he hadn't expected things to be this bad. The priest's letter had told of a mine filled with kidnapped Indians --- adults and kids both -- but it hadn't mentioned anything about the place being protected by a small army of paid cowboys.

"I believe it's all true," Wyatt replied softly. "This mine, though, it's like nothing I've ever heard of before."

"The Devil's Eye," Belle intoned. "You ask me, sounds like a might good name for that hellhole." She shrugged. "It don't matter to me what you all decide, I'm still going after my Sam. I'd never leave him alone to die in such a place."

"The same goes for my Frank," Annie said determinedly. "He's shot up, but if he's still alive then he deserves better than to be a slave in that mine."

"And the Apaches deserve their fate?" Geronimo said quietly.

"Relax, Goyathlay," Wyatt said, "nobody here's saying that. But we need to get inside before we can rescue anyone. I figure I know how to make that happen." He glanced over Cisco. "You've got that horse from those fellas we killed, right? So here's how it's going to play out   "

An hour later, just before midnight, the five of them reached the crest of a particularly steep bluff and found themselves looking down upon a small desert valley ringed on all sides by low, sharp peaks and plunging cliffs which were clearly impossible to navigate on foot or on horseback.

At the center of the valley, taking up most of the open space, was an enormous mesa nearly half a mile wide and hundreds of feet tall. The entire front of the formation was peppered with dozens of entrances which had been carved from the living rock.

Light spilled from most of them, creating a vast web of illumination that Wyatt might have considered beautiful had he not known what it signified. Even in the darkness and from several miles away, they could see thousands of men carrying torches up and down the vast, wood beam scaffolding that covered the enormous rock face.

"I'll be damned," Cisco whispered.

None of the rest of them said anything. They simply stared and tried to wrap their minds around what might await them in the depths of the mine.

"Just remember the plan," Wyatt said sharply, holding up his wrists, which were bound with a length of rope as all of theirs were. "Cisco here captured us, and he's bringing us in to the mine in exchange for the opportunity to join up."

"If you ask me, it isn't a very believable story," said Annie.

"Exactly what are you tryin' to say?" replied Cisco. "I could rope three just like you, little lady, and do it with one hand tied-"

"Goddamnit!" Wyatt interrupted, "I wish you two'd quit bickering. You're worse than a couple of old women. Once we ride down this mountain, we'll be riding right into one of their patrols. They hear us going

jawing like that and it could blow this whole plan straight to hell."

Wyatt urged his horse forward, keeping his bound hands on the saddle horn for balance. Annie, Belle, and Geronimo rode down behind him in a straight line. Cisco brought up the rear, a Winchester rifle resting diagonally across his lap.

The trail down to the valley was steep and difficult to navigate, and was covered by a slippery top layer of gravel. Wyatt suspected that it had been left that way on purpose to discourage unwanted visitors. There was most likely a better path elsewhere on the mountain, but it was probably only known to the men who lived and worked in the enormous mine.

As they descended further into the valley, the actual size and scope of the mesa quickly became apparent.

A narrow but swiftly-moving river encircled the base, creating a natural and highly effective moat which separated the mine from the rest of the valley floor. A single bridge, just wide enough for a single wagon and a couple of horses, had been built across the river. It appeared to be the only way to safely cross the swiftly moving current.

"All of you, halt right there," said a voice from out of the darkness and they all came to a stop. Wyatt heard the sound of a hammer being cocked, then another, and then another after that. It seemed that they

were surrounded.

"Hold up, now," Cisco called out, "these are my prisoners. I'm comin' to join up with y'all."

"Ain't no hiring going on here," said the voice, "and the ones coming to work ain't getting paid, stranger. Now drop that rifle and do it real slow."

"Now that don't seem hospitable at all," complained Cisco, allowing the Winchester to slide onto the ground. "Here I brung y'all some new hands and this is how I get paid for my trouble?"

"That surely is fucked up, ain't it," said the voice, and then Wyatt saw a man on a horse seem to rise up out of the ground to their right, emerging into the moonlight like one of Geronimo's spirits.

It took Wyatt a moment to realize that both horse and rider had been concealed in some kind of blind below ground level. The rider had his rifle trained on them, and when the other men rode into sight, he could see that they were all similarly armed.

"It sure is," Cisco said, raising his hands in the air. "Just so you boys know, I came here on good faith."

"That's the question, then, ain't it?" said the man, his rifle never wavering. "How'd you know we was here at all? We ain't exactly running ads in the newspaper."

"I came across a boy about a day's ride from here," Cisco said. "He was runnin' fast in the opposite

direction. Seemed to me he was tryin' to get as far away from here as he could."

"A boy," the first man said thoughtfully. "How old, abouts?"

"Fifteen, maybe sixteen."

The first man and one of the other riders exchanged glances. "Sounds like Baxter," the second man said. "Figured he'd turn tail and run sooner or later."

"Sure does look it," the first man replied. To Cisco, he said, "Maybe you did us a favor bringin' them in after all. But we'll have to let the boss decide what he wants to do with you."

With Cisco now a prisoner, the band of armed men led Wyatt and the others the rest of the way down the mountain and across the bridge. Up close, the river was wider and looked deeper than Wyatt had originally thought.

As they crossed the bridge, he took a closer look at the ripples caused by the current and felt his heart sink. If the bridge no longer became an escape option and they were forced to swim for it, things could get mighty uncomfortable for all of them. Once they were on the opposite side, the riders seemed to relax their guard a bit. Wyatt was certain, though, that any suspicious moves on their part would result swiftly in a bullet to the head.

As they approached the Devil's Eye, Wyatt could clearly see the large number of changes which had been made to the natural structure. The scaffolding was a hodgepodge of makeshift walkways, ladders, and ramps that had been built from the ground all the way to the top of the mesa more than two-hundred feet above the valley floor. Most of the caves they had seen from the bluff had actually been dynamited out of the living rock and were not naturally occurring.

Some of the openings were larger than others and were being used to bring the raw ore out of the depths of the mine. The riders herded them toward one cave that was especially large and uncharacteristically dark. Staring into the darkness, Wyatt felt dread begin to spread through his gut like a cancer. Fear was not an emotion he readily succumbed to, but it was hard not to be apprehensive when they knew nothing about what awaited them inside the mine.

Just before the mine engulfed them all, Wyatt looked back over his shoulder at the disappearing light. He hoped fervently, for all of their sakes, that he had not led them all to their deaths.

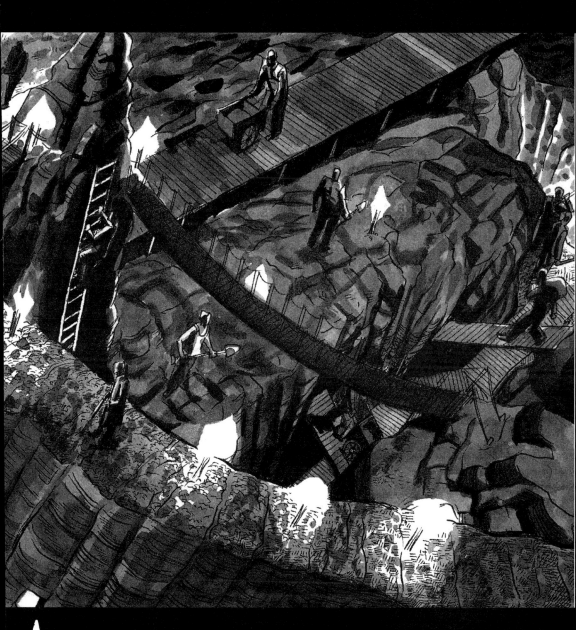

After proceeding through the black passages with a sense of purpose which suggested the men had done this many times before, the entire party turned a corner and emerged out of the darkness into a vast and bright cave which seemed almost as tall as the mesa itself.

The guards led them toward a large, two-story adobe structure which had been constructed in the center of the towering chamber. Several Indians were working in a small vegetable garden beside the front porch. At first they studied the newcomers with indifference, then they noticed Geronimo and their eyes widened in astonishment.

Geronimo pretended not to notice them and focused his eyes straight ahead. Wyatt had warned him that he might attract immediate attention and had told him to ignore it until told otherwise.

As he studied the adobe building, Wyatt decided this had to be the headquarters of whoever was in charge of the mine. The construction quality was top-notch; there were even rare glass panes set into the wood-frame windows. Then Wyatt saw the front door and his breath seemed to stop in his throat.

Carved into the wood was the flame-and-eye design that was the mark of the Devil's Eye mine.

This version had been created with the same exquisite care and craftsmanship as the tattoos and the stamp on Cisco's saddle holster. Unlike those others, however, this one had been painted in multiple shades of color and with great detail.

As they approached the building, the door opened. Not with any sense of urgency but leisurely, as if the building's occupant were coming out to greet a group of friendly visitors instead of prisoners most likely headed for a slow and agonizing death.

Whatever Wyatt was expecting from the man who ran the Devil's Eye, it was certainly not this. He was in his fifties at least, tall and surprisingly gaunt, with a sad and vaguely hangdog face which seemed, at first glance, to be on the verge of weeping. He was dressed in the clothes of a gentleman miner, and Wyatt noted with some surprise that his pants were perfectly creased and that his shirt appeared freshly laundered.

"Welcome to my house," the man said, moving farther out onto the porch. "You can all get down off your horses." His voice was deep and coarse, with the tenor of a man who had been a smoker most of his life.

It wasn't a request. The lead rider rode up beside the man and leaned down, whispering in this ear. The man nodded and then the rider wheeled his horse around and rode away without a backward glance.

Before the remaining two guards could force them to dismount, Wyatt swung his feet out of the stirrups and jumped to the ground. Behind him he could hear the others following suit.

Originally, his plan had been for them to join the mine's prisoners and ferment a revolt led by Geronimo and the imprisoned Indians. It was quickly becoming apparent, however, that the size and location of the Devil's Eye made it a highly effective jail. Getting out was going to take a bold and unexpected move on their part. Unfortunately, at that moment, Wyatt had no idea what that might be.

"Smitty tells me you brought these folks in and that you're looking for work," the man asked Cisco. "Is that true?"

Cisco nodded, but for once, had the good sense not to speak. The man glanced at Wyatt and his gaze seemed as deep and unfathomable as the river outside. "Do I know you?" he said after a moment. "Your face is familiar to me."

Wyatt saw no reason to lie. He knew this was not the sort of man who would be forgiving if he did. Their circumstances were dire enough without complicating things further.

"My name is Wyatt Earp," he replied. "Until a few days ago I was Marshall of Dodge City, Kansas."

"Is that a fact?" the man said, his eyebrows lifting in evident surprise. "You're a long way from home, Mr. Earp, and I must say, a highly improbable addition to my staff."

"Staff?" Wyatt said before he could stop himself. "Seems to me you're running a slave operation here, and from what I've heard, with men, women, and children alike."

"An emotional response," the man said with a shrug. "About what I expect from one of the Earp's I've heard so much about. Still, I won't deny your accusations." He studied Wyatt and then the others in turn. "Do all of you know who I am?"

"You're the bastard who took my Sam," Belle blurted out, her lips compressed by anger into a thin white line. "Other than that your name don't mean nothin' to me."

"I've taken no one," the man said mildly. "However, what my *men* may have done is something else

entirely. That, however, is not important. What *is* important is that you know who I am. My name is Harrison Kane, and as long as you are my guests, you'll do well to remember it." He turned his attention back to Wyatt. "Since your friends seem just as emotional as you, Mr. Earp, I'll let you finish the introductions."

"The one who brought us in is called the Cisco Kid," Wyatt said. "The little woman there is Annie Oakley and the taller one beside her goes by the name Belle Starr."

"And the Indian?" Kane asked.

"Goyathlay," Wyatt said automatically. He instinctively knew that now was not the time to identify

Geronimo by his white man's moniker and he hoped Kane did not know the famous Apache's given name. To Wyatt's great relief, Kane showed no reaction. In fact, he seemed more fascinated with their party as a whole than any one of them individually.

"This is quite a group," Kane said, studying them carefully as he paced slowly back and forth across the porch, "Quite a group, indeed."

The remaining guards shifted uneasily in their saddles. Wyatt sensed that Kane was not acting as he normally would toward a group of prisoners. This was making the guards nervous, and as a result Wyatt felt his own anxiety rising.

Although his head was barely moving, Cisco's eyes were flitting back and forth between Kane and the guards. Although he appeared relaxed, Wyatt knew better. If something didn't happen shortly, Cisco was going to act. If that happened, it was highly unlikely any of them would get out of this alive.

"We're just some folks thrown together by circumstance," Wyatt said, watching Kane carefully. "We're nothing special."

To his surprise, Kane simply smiled, revealing a set of teeth so white and straight that they might have been artificial.

"On the contrary, Mr. Earp," he said. "You're all very special. In fact, I'd say that odds of such a large and well-known group appearing on my doorstep all at once are fairly astronomical. It's enough to make a man believe Faro might be a winner's game after all."

"We just happened to be heading in the same direction," Wyatt said, and instantly regretted his words.

"Ah, yes," Kane said, his eyebrows lifting in mock surprise. "Now that's precisely my point, Mr. Earp. There are those odds again. I think we should discuss that a bit more." He nodded at the two remaining guards, who moved in closer to the other prisoners. "Why don't we go inside? We'll have a drink like civilized men and see if we can't arrive at some theory to explain all this."

Knowing that he had no other choice, Wyatt left the others behind and followed Kane past the elaborately carved door and into the shadowy interior of the building. After he had closed the door behind them, Kane led Wyatt into a spacious office off of the main hallway.

The room's decor clearly reflected the occupant's interest in history, although the density of the objects within seemed to suggest at least a degree of obsession. It seemed to Wyatt that the items had been chosen not out of respect for their origins, but for their desirability as possessions.

In addition to a small collection of European paintings, two on each wall, there was also a large and exquisite Navajo rug, half of which was concealed by matching leather chairs and an enormous wood desk

inlaid with elaborate carvings of eagles and other birds of prey. The remaining wall space was taken up by various pieces of antique Spanish armor including swords, helmets, and a battle-scarred breastplate, all gleaming as if carefully polished.

"Amazing, aren't they?" Kane said proudly as he pulled a concealed knife from behind his back and sliced off Wyatt's bindings with a single stroke. He indicated that Wyatt should sit down, but Wyatt declined. Kane shrugged. "Suit yourself."

Wyatt could think of nothing to say, because his mind was spinning. Other than the hidden knife, Kane appeared to be unarmed. Although Wyatt would have preferred a gun, one of the Spanish swords would serve just fine as a weapon — or Kane's knife, if he could get it away from him.

"They're quite old you know," Kane said, misinterpreting Wyatt's interest in the ancient weapons. He perched on the edge of his desk. "In fact, I'm fairly certain they were left by Francisco Coronado over three centuries ago. I found them in 1854, the day I first discovered this mesa and the remarkable caves within it. I've come to believe that Coronado and his men sought refuge in this valley after being attacked by one of

the early tribes of the region."

"Mighty short-sighted of them," Wyatt said dryly, "not wanting to be conquered the same way the Incas were."

"Conquerors or progressives," Kane said dismissively, "both are matters of perspective. The truth is, the natives of this country have been holding up progress for far too long. In fact, by my estimation the various warring tribes have delayed development in the southwestern desert states by as much as fifty years. Do you know what a tragedy that is, Mr. Earp?"

As he spoke, Kane used the tip of his knife to pick grit from beneath his fingernails. He clearly did not fear Wyatt's reputation, or at least believed that his being unarmed made him harmless. Hubris seemed to be one of Kane's larger flaws and Wyatt intended that it prove a fatal one.

When Wyatt moved, it was without warning or any hint of his intent. He reached the wall in two quick steps and pulled a Spanish short sword off of its mount.

Or tried to.

To Wyatt's surprise, his fingers slid off the pommel and he stumbled, nearly losing his balance. It appeared that the sword wasn't polished but rather coated with some kind of grease.

"A fine layer of gun oil," Kane said cheerfully, "carefully applied by one of my staff for situations precisely like this one. It never ceases to amaze me how predictable people are, Mr. Earp. Does it ever surprise you?"

Then, with the speed of a striking sidewinder, he hurled his blade with the unerring eye of a master knife thrower. Before Wyatt could dodge out of the way the blade sliced into his shoulder.

The pain was instantaneous and blinding. He immediately lost all feeling in his right arm as blood gushed out of the wound, soaking his shirt. Wyatt felt his legs weaken and groaned involuntarily as they began to give way.

This was not how it was supposed to happen, he thought. Not like this, not dying in some unknown mine, killed by a low-down no-good son-of-a-bitch like Harrison Kane.

This thought caused Wyatt to reach deep inside himself, to draw strength from the same reserve of iron-clad

will which had served him so many times in the past. Planting his left foot firmly in front of him, he used it to push himself upright-not all the way, but just enough to do what needed to be done.

Kane grinned as he watched Wyatt struggle to stay on his feet. "My only regret is that I'm going to have to commission another rug," he said, "since you've bled all over this one. Although perhaps I'll keep it, given that it's filled with the life's blood of the famous Wyatt Earp."

"You know," Wyatt gasped, gritting his teeth, "I'd have rather shot you. But this   this'll do just fine."

Then he reached up with his good arm and pulled the breastplate off of the wall. As he suspected, Kane had ordered that only the swords and knives be coated with gun oil. His arrogance had never allowed him to consider the idea of someone using an unconventional object like the breastplate for a weapon.

Lurching forward, Wyatt swung the armor into Kane's face with all of his strength. The force of the blow shattered Kane's nose and knocked him backward across the desk, unconscious.

The enormous effort was more than Wyatt's weakened body could take. He allowed the breastplate to slide from his almost nerveless fingers as he slumped to the floor. Leaning back against the front of the desk,

he closed his eyes and breathed heavily, trying to regain some of his lost strength.

Reaching up, he pulled the knife from his shoulder. As he sat there feeling fresh blood flowing from the wound and down his side, Wyatt was tempted to rest for a moment, to let Geronimo and the rest of them finish this thing.

Then he thought of Mattie back in Dodge City, who for better or for worse was his responsibility. And what of Geronimo, Annie, Belle, and Cisco? He'd led them here and he was damned sure going to see them through it, one way or the other. There was also the issue of Father Pedro and the captive Indians which had started this whole damn thing in the first place.

Cursing the priest for what seemed like the hundredth time in as many days, Wyatt struggled to his feet. Hefting the bloody knife, he strode out of the office and down the hallway. Pausing in front of the door, he took a deep breath, then threw it open and stepped out onto the porch.

When Wyatt appeared out of the depths of the house, pale skinned, soaked in blood, and wielding Kane's knife, he must have seemed to the Indians like some avenging spirit. They gasped in fear and threw themselves facedown in the furrows.

The two remaining guards froze, staring at Wyatt in disbelief. He knew that men of their ilk almost always knew of him, if only by reputation. More than a few such men had met the butt of his Navy revolver while drunk on the streets of Dodge City. Still, the sight of him bloody, his face a mask of rage and determination, seemed to have paralyzed them.

Wyatt took in the scene at a glance. Then, with the last of his fading strength, he threw Kane's knife at the nearest guard. The blade closed the gap in the blink of an eye and caught the man in the side of the neck. Gagging on his own blood, he dropped his rifle and slumped out of the saddle. Even as he died, his fingers still fumbled at his throat in a useless attempt to stop his life from draining away.

Shaken by what he had just witnessed, the second guard began to bring his rifle to bear. And that's when Geronimo struck.

With a heart-stopping war cry, Geronimo leapt from a standing position and knocked the guard off of the horse before he could fire. Even with his hands tied, the Apache was still a formidable warrior. Utilizing the force of his charge and his own weight, he grabbed the top of the guard's head and twisted it, breaking the man's neck with an audible crack.

Without hesitation, Geronimo rolled to his feet and snatched up the guard's rifle, taking aim at several guards who were running toward them from one of the nearby caves. His first shot, fired from the waist, took down one of them. He fired two more times in rapid succession, bringing down the other two before they could get off a single shot.

Belle pulled the knife from the dead guard's neck and used it to cut away everyone's ropes. Pulling a roll of clean cloth from his saddlebag, Cisco bandaged Wyatt's injury while Geronimo and Annie laid down covering fire.

Despite the chaos which had erupted around them, the two Indians remained facedown in the dirt, either in terror or in an attempt to avoid being hit by stray bullets. Geronimo called out in Apache, "Get up, brothers! Now is the time to fight!"

The older of the two rose hesitantly to his knees and nodded at Geronimo. "Aye, Goyathlay," he replied proudly in Apache, "it is true that we are your brothers, and we are ready to fight with you!"

"Our freedom is near," Geronimo said. "Do not fail me." He turned back to Wyatt. "We have only these two rifles," he said. "They will not be enough to win this battle."

"No," Wyatt said, nodding toward the guards that Geronimo had shot, "but those rifles will help. Get your two 'brothers' there to pick 'em up and we'll be a sight better off than we are now."

More guards began to emerge from the various cave entrances. Some of them began to fire on the pueblo from the higher levels, throwing up small funnels of sand around Wyatt and the others.

"We need to get under cover," Wyatt said. "If we try to hide in the pueblo, we're done for. They'll surround us and burn us out if they have to."

"What of Kane?" Geronimo asked. He chambered his rifle and fired at a guard partially concealed behind a third-level balustrade overlooking the pueblo.

The question was a good one. Wyatt's original plan had been to simply kill him, using his death to demoralize the guards until Wyatt and the others could establish some kind of control over the Devil's Eye

mine. However, now he had a better idea one that might just get them all out of this alive and put an end to Kane's operation once and for all.

"Come on," he said to Geronimo, "help me get Kane out of the house and onto a horse."

"What're you doing, Wyatt?" Cisco said. "We've gotta get *out* of the open, not the other way around!"

"I don't have the time to explain everything to you," Wyatt said. "So why don't you stop yapping and help Geronimo and me get Kane tied up?"

"We'll keep them back for now," Annie said firmly. "You all do what you need to." She and Belle crouched down beside the porch, firing with deadly accuracy whenever a guard was careless enough to show himself.

I sure as hell hope you know what you're doing," Cisco muttered as the three of them hurried inside.

They found Kane exactly as Wyatt had left him. Twin ribbons of scarlet were trickling from his ruined nose, but not nearly enough to satisfy Wyatt. He was lightheaded from blood loss and the effect made him aware of just how close he had come to dying at the hands of Harrison Kane. The temptation to just kill the man then and there was great; but Wyatt had never been the kind of man to kill another in cold blood, and he wasn't about to start now.

"You two get him tied up," Wyatt said.

"And then what?" Cisco said irritably. "You plannin' on mountin' him on your wall like one of these old swords?"

"No such thing," Wyatt said, moving around to the back of the desk and going through the various drawers. After a moment he found what he was looking for: a Merwin-Hulbert .44 caliber revolver. The elaborate nickel-plated design and ivory grips were a bit ostentatious for Wyatt's taste, but he figured any gun was better than none at all, especially under the circumstances.

"That's it?" Cisco said, staring at Wyatt. "Just, 'no such thing'? That's all you're gonna say?"

"Goddamnit," Wyatt snapped, "you are a pain in my ass, Cisco. We're going to use Kane there to get us the hell out of here. Now is that good enough for you?"

"It is not as honorable as simply cutting his throat," Geronimo said after locating some rope in another room and typing Kane up like a prize hog. "But it will do."

Throwing Kane over his shoulder with the same ease that some men would a sack of grain, Geronimo followed Wyatt and Cisco outside. The two Indians set down their newly captured rifles long enough to help

Geronimo secure Kane on a horse, his body upright and his arms securely tied.

"Now I need you to get their attention," Wyatt told Geronimo. "We're going to end this here and now."

Geronimo nodded and stepped into the open. Holding his rifle over his head, he screamed another war cry. It seemed to shake the very foundations of the ancient mesa, and for a moment, all noise ceased. Then Wyatt stepped up beside him and shouted as hard as he could, hoping that the guards would hear him and repeat what he had to say to the others who could not.

"Everybody hold their fire! I mean everybody! We have Kane and if anybody fires a single shot I'll put a bullet through his head sure as hell! So whoever your leader is, send 'em down now!"

At first there was no response, but Wyatt considered it a good sign that nobody shot at them. Then a voice called out, "How do we know you won't plug anybody we send out there?"

Wyatt took a deep breath. He thought about what Kane had asked, if people still surprised him. In all honesty, very few things surprised him anymore except stupidity. That seemed to be an essential law of the universe, as timeless as a block of granite and just about as intractable. Still, pointing out to the unseen speaker how dumb his question was would accomplish nothing.

"I guarantee it with my word," Wyatt yelled back. "My name's Earp, and some of you might know me by reputation. If you know my name, then you know what my word is worth!"

After just a few moments, a single figure stepped out of one of the nearest caves, his hands up indicating that he was unarmed. He was tall and stocky, with graying brown hair and eyes that were both shrewd and cautious. When he had approached to within a dozen yards of where Geronimo and Wyatt were standing, he nodded briefly and glanced at Kane's unconscious figure.

"He dead or just knocked out?"

"He's out," Wyatt said, "but he isn't dead. Not yet, anyway."

"It is," Wyatt said, "and the big Indian here is Geronimo."

"How in the hell—" the man said, then stopped in mid-sentence and grinned humorlessly. "It don't matter no-how. If anyone was going to show up here with Geronimo, I suppose an Earp is as good as anybody. Or should I call you *Marshall* Earp?"

"I'm not wearing a badge," Wyatt said, "not this time. I'm here looking for a friend, and for that matter,

a few of his friends, too."

"So if we give up your friends, you'll leave?" The man's grin never wavered. "That seems mighty unlikely."

"Not much chance of that," Wyatt agreed. "Even if I find my friend, this mine's done for. I'll see to that. And if I don't, then Geronimo or the rest of 'em I came with sure as hell will."

"Seems we've got nothing to lose here, then," the man said. "Might just be in our best interest to storm Kane's pueblo and take our chances."

"Maybe so," Wyatt said. "Or maybe I've got a better idea. You and your men ride out of here and don't look back. There's been enough killing and maiming and God only knows what else in this hellhole. You all ride out now and I'm not likely to come looking for you."

"And what about the Eye?" the man said, gesturing with one of his upraised hands to take in the enormity of their surroundings. "What'll happen to it? You get rid of Kane and somebody else'll just come along and take over where he left off. There's still enough silver left over in this place to make a man mighty rich. "

"I think I know what to do about that, too," Wyatt said. "When I'm done here there won't be anything left to take over. You've got my word on that."

Staring into Wyatt's face, the man considered his words. Then he nodded slowly. "Okay," he said, "you've got yourself a deal. We ride, all of us. No names and you'll make sure no one else comes back to this valley?"

"I'll do that and more," Wyatt replied.

Nodding his assent, the man turned and started to walk away. Then he paused and turned back to look at them. "I was paid real well here," he said, "but something about it never did sit right with me. I think it was the priest that finally did it. Putting the heathens to work seemed the natural thing to do, but white men were something else altogether."

Wyatt felt Geronimo stiffen beside him and held up his hand to stop the Apache from doing something rash.

"Is the priest still alive?" Wyatt asked.

"Yep." The man nodded. "He's in the barracks, didn't have the strength to work in the mine. We had him taking care of the sick heathens instead."

"Then it's time you and your boys got moving," Wyatt said. "And my advice is that you don't look back, not a one of you."

Clearing out the Devil's Eye took the better part of a week. The guards had left-the majority of them agreeably--but a few decided to try and take back the mine anyway. With most of their fellow guards already gone and those rifles now in the hands of their former prisoners, the uprising was over before it had really begun.

Wyatt found father Pedro exactly where he had been told, caring for the sick and dying victims of Harrison Kane's silver mining ambitions. He was pale and dirty, and after his time in the mine, much thinner than Wyatt remembered. Still, he seemed unsurprised that Wyatt had come for him.

"My son, the only question I have," Father Pedro said as they walked across the bridge together, "is what took you so long?"

They were following a line of wagons carrying the litters of those final few who were too weak or infirm to walk out of the Devil's Eye on their own two feet.

"Despite what you seem to think," Wyatt said, pausing to glance down at the swiftly moving river,

"I do have a thing or to that takes up my time."

"Of course you do, my son," Father Pedro said in the same calm, measured voice that Wyatt had always found infuriatingly smug.

"I'm glad we agree on something," Wyatt said. "Far as I'm concerned, this settles my debt to you. Can we at least agree on that?"

Once they were on the opposite bank the two men turned and stared up at the now silent and

abandoned mine.

"Life is such a rare and wonderful thing, Wyatt," Father Pedro replied solemnly, although his eyes seemed to twinkle in the fading afternoon light. "I think you will agree that one cannot put a price on something so precious."

Then he turned and walked away, leaving Wyatt speechless with frustration. Geronimo came across the bridge a moment later and studied the priest's retreating back. "Your Father Pedro is a good man," he said. "He has saved many lives in this place, not just those of my people, but yours, as well."

"Yeah," Wyatt said, "he's a real prince among men."

What he didn't say was that some part of him wished the priest had been captured *before* he'd managed to get off the letter to Wyatt. It would have made his life a whole hell of a lot easier.

"Few men can make that claim," Geronimo said, missing Wyatt's sarcasm–or deliberately ignoring it. Wyatt couldn't tell which.

"Is it done?" Wyatt asked, shading his eyes.

"These are the last of the workers," Geronimo said. "With Cisco's help, we were able to make use of all

the explosives."

"Then let's get the hell out of here," Wyatt said, "and blow this place to kingdom come."

Gathering up a pair of horses, Wyatt and Geronimo rode out of the valley behind the last of the wagons. Cisco rode beside them, laying out blasting fuse as they went. When they finally joined Annie and Belle on the ridge overlooking the Devil's Eye, the sun was near the horizon and half of the mesa was draped in the shadows of the impending night.

Behind them, Sam Starr sat with Annie's husband, Frank. He was recovering, but owed his life to Father Pedro's care. According to Annie, their plan was to continue building up their sharpshooting act until they had enough saved to buy a ranch. From what Wyatt had seen of Annie, he had no doubt that they would succeed at whatever they decided to do.

Belle and Sam were clearly in love, but they didn't seem to care much about what happened to the Devil's Eye now that Sam was free. Wyatt knew that both of them were about as different from Annie and Frank as the night was from the day. Belle was a unique and single-minded woman ~ not to mention one hell of a shot. But there was a blackness in them both that did not bode well for a hopeful future, and Wyatt

suspected he would not see them again. Wyatt forced Kane to sit on his horse, watching as Cisco hooked up the fuses to the firing plunger.

"You don't have to do this," Kane said, "there's a fortune still down in that mine. I'll share it with all of you."

"Mister, do all of us a favor and shut up," Annie said, "your tongue's as forked as a Western Diamondback's and I'm sick of hearing it flapping around."

Suddenly, as if galvanized by the sight of his mine about to be destroyed, Kane threw off the ropes binding his hands. Clearly he had been working at them for some time, waiting until just the right moment for escape presented itself.

His unexpected action caught Wyatt and Geronimo by surprise. They both reached for the guns. Annie turned and scrambled for her own, which was leaning against her wagon just out of reach. Before any of them could bring their weapons to bear, Cisco turned and fired, drawing his gun so fast that Wyatt saw little more than a blur. His bullet caught Kane in the center of his forehead, leaving a nearly bloodless hole so neat that it might have been painted there.

Then Kane fell face down in the sand. His right foot shook for a moment, then was still.

"That was mighty fast," Wyatt said appreciatively, allowing his own Navy Colt to slide back into its holster.

"Told you I was quick," Cisco said, grinning widely. "Ain't nobody faster'n me, not even Wyatt Earp."

Wyatt started to say something, but then thought better of it. "You know something, Cisco, you may be right. Now let's blow this thing so we can all head home."

When Cisco pushed the plungers, the ground seemed to lift beneath their feet for a moment before settling back down again. A series of titanic explosions erupted inside the Devil's Eye, sending massive clouds of dirt and dust billowing out of the mesa's many cave entrances. The thick haze temporarily blocked out the sun before finally settling back to earth.

Wyatt found himself looking down on a new mountain, one hewn not by the power of God but by the hand of man. Having collapsed in upon itself, nothing but rubble remained to mark the spot where Harrison Kane had wrought such misery. Even the river itself had ceased to flow, its path broken by the many tons of debris which now covered the majority of the valley floor.

"May such an evil place never again exist," Father Pedro said softly.

"Amen to that," Cisco said.

Not much chance of that," Wyatt said softly. "There will always be places like this. Don't you know that, Father?"

"Here's to hoping not," Annie said. "After all, hope is all we've got, Wyatt."

"Perhaps," Geronimo said, "that will be enough."

Overhead the night's first stars flickered in the twilight sky. Somewhere in the distance thunder rolled, signaling the coming of yet another storm.

Behind them, the Devil's Eye lay blinded, its evil stilled forever. The only evidence that it had existed at all was the unmarked grave of Harrison Kane.

Thankfully, Wyatt knew, even that would disappear with time.

THE END

WYATT EARP

Wyatt Earp, who shares the namesake, bloodline and wanderlust of the famed western lawman, embraced his heritage at an early age. The son of Henry Lee Earp, an oilfiled driller, horseman and Baptist deacon, he quickly learned skills with guns, horses and the land at his rural Oklahoma home. While other kids were shooting BB's and riding bikes, he was driving tractors, tending animals, building fence and killing varmints. Historically important bloodlines run deep on both sides of the family. His great grandfather Merrill invented the first 4 point barbed wire ever mass produced in the American West and his Mother Wanda's lineage is traced back to the Mayflower pilgrims.

Most actors grow up wanting to be cowboys, Wyatt grew up a cowboy wanting to be an actor. His plan at age 8 was to become the next matt Dillon of *Gunsmoke* fame, figuring that by the time he reached adulthood, Hollywood might be ready to replace James Arness. His show and tell would always involve episodes of *Gunsmoke* written by, starring and directed by Wyatt Earp. Since there was no theater or acting class anywhere near his town he decided to put those dreams on hold. He went on to be a high achiever in High School, worked his way through college, served as a missionary to Africa for a summer and began full time work as an investment broker during his senior year at Oklahoma State University (The Cowboys of course). Shortly after graduation he became the youngest Republican county chairman in Oklahoma history and was recruited to run for public office. However, the oil bust was on and he had unfinished business and bigger dreams to take care of in Hollywood.

In January 1988 he arrived in Los Angeles with a T -Bird full of clothes and a wallet full of nothing. In short order though, he became a successful mortgage broker. This career would serve him well for years to come and help him to avoid ever having a single stint as a waiter while pursuing his ambitions and dreams in the entertainment field.

After learning his craft, acting in several student films and a short film, it was his casting in the film *Tombstone* that gave Wyatt his first big break. While he was on set for 4 months, playing a character named Billy Claibourne (famous for running out of the OK corral gunfight) he received a great deal of on the job training and advice from the likes of Sam Elliott, Kurt Russell and Val Kilmer. The final edit of the movie left his role and seemingly his career on the cutting room floor. It seemed for a great many casting directors, a guy named Wyatt Earp was suspect. Sam Elliott stood up for his credibility though, in a *People* magazine interview in which Sam said " Look him in the eye and you know he's not a joke". Thanks Sam.

In spite of the good publicity, after losing his agent to a heart attack and the following one to a self inflicted gunshot wound, Wyatt determined that perhaps his timing was not right. So once again, he his attention to several successful business ventures. His mortgage business is now conducted at his firm, Wyatt Earp Capital Group Inc. He is also the CEO of Compassionate Technologies, a medical device firm who's proprietary and breakthrough technology, THE HOT IV (which he co-invented) is poised to launch later this year.

In 2007 Wyatt re-kindled his efforts as an artist and has been cast as a Sheriff Danford, a series regular in a project entitled Sordid Lives. He has created two scripted series which are in development with major independent production companies. He has also returned to booking work as a voice over artist. Perhaps in 2008 the timing will be right for this modern day Wyatt Earp in the entertainment business   if he can find a healthy agent.